# MEGAN'S CHOICE

DARCI GARCIA

5 PRINCE PUBLISHING

Published by 5 PRINCE PUBLISHING & BOOKS, LLC

PO Box 865, Arvada, CO 80001

www.5PrinceBooks.com

ISBN digital: 978-1-63112-278-1

ISBN print: 978-1-63112-351-1

Cover Credit: Marianne Nowicki

*To my mother, Elnora Ellsworth Halstead. My greatest champion, my most stalwart defender, my best friend. How do I thank one such as you? I cannot. This is all I have, Mom, and I offer it humbly, with reverence and with every ounce of love that I have.*

# ACKNOWLEDGMENTS

A very special thank you to my husband, Tony, for his unfailing support and unconditional love.

My son, Erik, for his honest critiques, for honoring and respecting me always, and for believing that his imperfect mother is perfectly wonderful.

My friends and family for their unwavering faith that this day would come, especially my circle of empowering females; Elena, Lindsey, Alice, Emily, Evelyn, Eva, Raeann. You have made this journey so much more and I love you all.

Lucy. My beautiful girl, my most precious companion. What I wouldn't give to find you, just one last time, under the bed with my shoe in your mouth.

Lastly, I would like to acknowledge my tiniest cheerleader, but by far the loudest; Piper, I know that you will change the world. You have already changed mine.

# MEGAN'S CHOICE

# CHAPTER 1

Megan slid her upper torso slightly forward, shimmying as she worked herself further under the bed, her cheek skimming along the hardwood floor. Flipping back an errant blonde strand, she finally spied her prey, just out of reach. Stretching out her arm, fingers fully extended, she was mere millimeters away.

"Are you kidding me?" she mumbled, blowing a ball of dust out of the way. Dark eyes stared back from a broad, black muzzle sprouting fuzzy white patches. The flat black nose, surrounded by deep folds only added character to the obstinate disposition of its owner.

"Lucy, I mean it," Megan hissed, "come out right now." The muzzle in question belonged to Megan's Boston terrier. Currently, Lucy was holding Megan's favorite slingback shoe hostage, something she tended to do. It now dangled precariously between her large pink jowls.

"Want a cookie?" she asked, desperately. She hated to reward bad behavior with a treat but, let's face it, she thought, everyone does it. A blink of bright expressive eyes marked her reaction, as slobber slowly rolled off the destroyed shoe onto the floor.

Scooting back out, Megan stood, making a mental note to clean under the bed as she brushed the dirt off her shirt.

Entering her small kitchen, she grabbed one of Lucy's favorite snacks, then rushing back, knelt, placing the dog biscuit just past the edge of the bed. Leaning back on her heels, Megan waited. Predictably, within just a few seconds she heard a rustling sound along with the tap-tap of nails as Lucy made her way towards her treat. Peeking her head out, she gazed longingly at her bribe, her eyes darting between the prize and Megan's face. Placing her hand out, Megan simply stared at Lucy until finally, the mangled shoe slid from her jaws. Springing forward, she joyfully grabbed the treat, her hind end swaying happily as she made her way to her soft bed to savor the spoils. Sighing loudly, Megan observed the destroyed shoe, one of her favorites. They weren't too high or too low, she reflected sadly. Just the perfect in-between. Grasping it gingerly to avoid most of the saliva, she carried it to the kitchen trash, and giving it one last regretful glance, she tossed it in. Checking her watch, she hurried to find an alternate pair from her now depleted shoe rack. Glancing over her shoulder as she made her way back to her bedroom, she observed Lucy happily chomping away, the victor with her spoils. Smiling, Megan shook her head slightly, revisiting in her mind the day she had found her unruly dog.

It had been raining heavily, a gloomy afternoon in the quaint city of Bath, a small town located in Maine, just thirty minutes outside of Portland. Megan had been staring out the large window of her flower shop, contemplating the dismal day. On a whim she decided to close early. It had been busy, despite the weather, with excellent sales so she didn't feel too guilty calling it a day.

Megan had been saving since starting her first job working concessions at a movie theatre, even managing to get her business degree with no student loans. Working two jobs and studying had been the hardest thing she had ever done but ultimately, she had graduated, spending the next five years managing various businesses in preparation for opening her own store. Driven by her love of nature as well as a fierce desire to be the master of her destiny, she was finally able to open her flower shop. A bonus was its convenient location to an apartment complex within walking distance where she was able to rent while saving to buy her own home. Grabbing her umbrella, Megan had decided to brave the rain and head out. As she began hurrying down the sidewalk, she observed something black up ahead, huddled against the wall of another storefront. Blinking against the drops in her eyes, Megan could see it was a small dog, completely soaked, shivering and emaciated. As she approached, the exhausted creature looked at her, eyes sunken, brimming with pain and suffering. Raw empathy coursed through Megan. With no thought to the consequences, she knelt, placing her hand gently on top of its shaking head.

"You poor thing," she murmured, as she had leaned forward to better inspect the fragile creature. On closer examination, Megan could see it was a female. How could anyone abandon an innocent animal, she wondered, anger coursing through her.

"Well little one," she whispered softly as she carefully gathered the dog up, "it looks like it's you and me from now on." When their eyes met, Megan knew immediately that they were meant for each other. She had posted flyers in case the bedraggled puppy had belonged to someone who had simply lost the tiny canine, but no one came forward to claim her. Finally, Megan truly knew that the precious stray was home forever and decided, after some consideration, to name the pup, Lucy.

"I think it suits you," Megan told Lucy one evening, as the two snuggled on the couch. "Small, pretty and compact." They had settled in happily with each other and soon Megan couldn't remember a time that her hellion canine had not been a part of her life. Lucy even went to work with Megan every day, acquiring many adoring fans amongst the flower shop's clientele.

The only downside had turned out to be the effect on Megan's love life.

There had been several boyfriends, but Lucy had made it quite clear that she didn't like any of them. In fact, they were sure to be the recipient of her special brand of bullying that included a determined glare, a threatening growl and for added effect, she would occasionally even bare her teeth. Ultimately, her guest would make a hasty retreat. Their behavior was completely understandable, however, there was the hopelessly romantic part of her that felt the right man could win her self-charged protector over.

If not, I will just remain single, she thought, or maybe start adding some cats? Shaking her head, she dismissed the idea. Too soon, she assured herself. Still, Megan was fine with being unattached. At just twenty-eight she was in no hurry for marriage. One day she would like to find love, the kind that ended in a genuine happily ever after, yet there was a part of her that wasn't entirely sure she would recognize if it even did happen. So far no one had ever given her the shivers. She had read about that once in a particularly steamy romance novel and it had stuck with her. Still, she thought, I may not be deliriously happy, but I am reasonably content.

Her parents, Elizabeth and Douglas Cunningham, lived close by as did her younger sister Lindsey, and they visited each other often. Lindsey would spend occasional nights over, the two women frequently lying awake in bed talking and giggling into the wee hours with Lucy nestled between them, snoring softly. Megan's best friend Gabby was also a regular visitor, although, having married last year they didn't see each other as much as they used to. Megan had found the announcement of Gabby's engagement bittersweet. She knew that although they would always be close, things would change, and Megan couldn't help but feel sorrowful at the loss of that special time in their lives. Feeling a nudge on the small of her back, Megan turned from her kneeling position in front of her closet. Lucy stood; her leash clenched in her mouth.

"Ok," Megan laughed. Choosing a pair of flats, she stood up. "I know, I know, it's time to go." Sliding into her shoes, she quickly snapped on Lucy's leash. Grabbing her purse along with Lucy's dog bag off the counter, they headed out. Stepping into the hallway, she marveled once again at the choice of carpeting that ran the length of the long corridor. Its spiral circles in bright oranges and deep blue always made her a little dizzy. As Megan turned to make her way to the elevator, she noticed activity several doors down. Men wearing polo shirts that read *We Move Everything* were busy carrying boxes into the empty apartment. Must be a new neighbor moving in, she thought. Suddenly, Lucy began pulling on her leash while Megan kept trying to gently wrest her back, however, she seemed unusually fascinated by the movers.

"Lucy, stop," Megan commanded. Normally the dog trotted directly to the elevator, never interested in any of the residents, even when they tried to pet her. Suddenly, Megan felt the leash go lax, then watched as it dropped away from the harness. She realized too late that she had not secured it properly. Sensing she was free, Lucy sprang forward.

"Lucy no," Megan scolded, chasing her down the hallway. With a sinking sensation, she watched as her disobedient dog veered sharply right, into the empty unit. Panicked, Megan reached the open door. Just as she was about to enter, she crashed headlong into a chest. A very large, very male chest. Immediately a strong hand grasped her shoulder, helping to steady her as she rocked back from the impact. Breathless, she looked up. The stranger's eyes were startling, an icy blue mixed with slate. Extraordinary, she thought, fascinated by their hue.

"Are you ok?" the man asked, his brow furrowed in concern.

"What?" Megan stuttered, staring up at him, completely unable to form a cohesive thought. This is exactly why you're still single, she thought, still mute. Just then Lucy began barking furiously. Horrified, Megan observed her errant dog run deliriously over the stranger's very expensive leather couch. Her tongue hung almost to her feet as she trailed drool joyously. The man had turned away from her, staring incredulously.

"Is that your dog?" he asked without turning.

"That dog?" Megan squeaked. "No. I mean yes, yes of course she is," then, pushing past the stranger, Megan ran towards Lucy who wasn't the least bit concerned by the murderous look on Megan's face. Instead, she proceeded to jump from the couch to a large, overstuffed chair. There, Lucy grabbed a bright yellow throw pillow that had been resting on the arm, simultaneously chewing and tossing it from side to side. Horrified, Megan stood rooted as her mind tried to absorb the sheer lunacy of this moment.

"Please drop the pillow, please, please," she repeated, under her breath. By now, Megan was praying for the floor to open up and swallow her whole. That or instant death. Either would work, she thought, practically panting with embarrassment. Her silk shirt had slipped out of her waistband, and when she had lunged for Lucy, she lost a shoe. They were her slightly too big ones that she had been forced to wear due to her devil canine. By now, Megan was sweating profusely, her distress hovering somewhere in the acute range. I must look simply stunning, she thought hysterically, still very much aware of the gorgeous male watching the destruction of his personal property unfold. Grabbing the pillow, Megan pulled it, still attached to Lucy, towards her. Just as her finger was about to slide under the collar bearing the name of that worthless puppy training school, she heard a terrible ripping sound, accompanied by a cloud of exploding white feathers. Excited, Lucy let go of the pillow, jumping to the floor as she chased the floating white creatures in circles. Both Megan and Lucy were covered in the white plumage, small pieces of yellow fabric mixed in. Megan watched in shocked fascination as the carnage floated onto the stranger's floor, her stomach sinking to somewhere under her feet.

Just as Megan was about to begin the chase again, Lucy was swept off the floor into the arms of the blue-eyed man. Immediately, she slowed her panting, quickly dragging her dangling tongue back into her mouth, her eyes fixed adoringly on him. Lucy appeared to be listening intently, her head cocked slightly, large ears standing straight up, as the stranger murmured sweet nothings to her. Megan instantly started forward to take her when Lucy licked his face once, then proceeded to rest her quill-strewn head in the crook of his neck. Dumbfounded, Megan could only stare. Lucy had never exhibited such immediate fondness for anyone else, not even her sister, Lindsey or her parents who doted on her. Yet clearly, she felt something special for this man. Well, Megan thought, not only was she a shoe carnivore, she was clearly also a traitor.

Walking forward, Megan was encouraged by the stranger's smile. He had flawlessly straight, white teeth and Megan couldn't help but notice the tiny crow's feet by his almond shaped eyes, that had no doubt been placed ever so perfectly, by his own personal angel on high. His hair was kohl black, smoothed back and very thick. Upon closer inspection she observed, as well, his commanding bone structure framed by a square, even brow. His nose ended in a blunt plane rather than a point which only enhanced his rugged good looks. Noting how gently he held Lucy, something inside of Megan warmed.

"I cannot apologize enough—" she began, but the dog whisperer interrupted.

"I hated that pillow anyway," he replied laughingly. "I will assume that this beauty is Lucy. It was the name you were yelling," he finished, clearly amused.

"The one and only," Megan affirmed, still working through ten levels of embarrassment. She could feel the sweat on her brow but refused to further humiliate herself by attempting to wipe it with the sleeve of her silk blouse, "Mutilator of shoes and —at the risk of getting too personal—the queen of flatulence."

Too much information, she thought, wincing inwardly. Reaching forward, Megan took Lucy from the man, placing her gently on the floor as she reattached her leash. Glancing around at the chaos, Megan spied her shoe. Attempting to maintain what shreds of dignity remained, she limped majestically over to retrieve it. Sliding it on, she then tucked in her shirt. Finally dressed, she reached out her hand.

"I'm Megan Cunningham," she announced, "I live a few doors down, which may or may not cause you to reconsider your choice of apartment complex."

Laughing, he shook her hand firmly. "Brice Castillo," he offered, his eyes intense as they moved over her. Megan felt her heart begin to beat not so much faster but harder, the sensation leaving her slightly breathless. Megan allowed herself a leisurely moment to examine the male specimen before her. He was very tall, possibly more than six feet, she observed. His white shirt hugged his shoulders and arms, and Megan could see the muscles that flexed when he moved. His jeans, slightly faded, stretched over thighs that were thick and powerful. He was barefoot, which for some strange reason, caused Megan's respirations to tick up a few notches. It had not escaped her notice—because she purposely looked—that his left hand was devoid of a wedding ring. Suddenly feeling magnanimous, she smiled down at Lucy warmly, her eyes slowly widening in horror when she realized there was a small puddle forming around her. Heart plummeting, she closed her eyes briefly, silently shaking her fist at the fates.

"Lucy, no!" Megan cried. Glancing down, Brice quickly grabbed a roll of paper towels resting on the kitchen counter and before Megan could help, he bent, quickly wiping the floor himself.

"That's it," Megan stated, her face beet red, "we are leaving before she destroys something else. Again, I am so sorry for everything." Glancing down at Lucy's angelic face, she continued, "I have no idea what has gotten into her. I mean she's usually so good, and well, I'm just really sorry..." she finished breathlessly, furiously brushing feathers off her shirt. Waving away her apology, Brice threw the wet towels away and after quickly rinsing his hands, followed Megan and Lucy as they made their way to the door. Stepping into the hall, Megan turned, placing her hand out once again.

"Please, at least let me replace your pillow," Megan began, but Brice shook his head.

"That won't be necessary," he assured her, sending Lucy a gentle smile. "It was wonderful to meet you both and I certainly hope we see each other again." Bending, he patted Lucy's head as she looked up at him rapturously. Good grief, Megan thought, she is really laying it on thick. "Maybe after the rest of my furniture arrives?"

Flustered, Megan replied. "Yes, I would like that. I'm just down the hall in unit B."

Taking a deep breath, she gave a half wave as she turned, heading once more towards the elevator, mentally scolding herself for her awkwardness. He probably thinks I'm a lunatic, she thought, resisting the urge to turn around. Megan could feel his eyes on her back and was relieved when she finally heard his door close. That went well, she thought, wiping sweat from her forehead. Welcome to the neighborhood.

# CHAPTER 2

*C*losing the door, Brice turned, slowly taking stock of the collateral damage left behind by Lucy. He stood for a few moments, his hands in his pants pockets, smiling. He still wasn't exactly sure what had happened, however, the remaining impression he had was less about the dog than it was about her owner. Certainly no one could have prepared him for the petite beauty that had so gloriously careened into him.

He first noticed her eyes, an unusual shade of amber, tossed with miniature flecks of gold. Her body, for the few sublime seconds it rested against his, was decidedly curvy in all the right places. Instantly, he felt his body tighten in response. Taking his hands out of his pockets, he shook his head, surprised by the power of his need. As he began sweeping up the feathers, along with the shredded pieces of pillow, he couldn't help but chuckle at the image of Megan limping, as gracefully as she could, to retrieve her lost shoe. Despite the chaos, Brice had been unable to take his eyes off her, not even when Lucy had been grappling with the ugly yellow pillow, a housewarming gift from his sister. He thought that he really should thank Lucy for that as he tossed the last of the debris into the trash. Finally finished, he sat, waiting for the mysteriously disappeared movers to return. It certainly was an unusual welcome to the neighborhood, he thought, smiling crookedly.

Originally born and raised in Miami, he had decided after graduating and fulfilling his internship to accept an offer here in Maine. Brice loved winter sports and preferred the change of seasons allowed, but he would miss his friends, as well as his sister who worked in Orlando. Hearing a knock, Brice jumped up, then crossing to the door quickly flung it open. Surprised, the mover stepped back, his expression startled. Oh, sorry, Brice mumbled, trying not to show his disappointment. He had hoped it was her. Brice forced himself to dwell on anything else except the beautiful woman who had literally careened into his life but found himself unable to stop thinking about her. He wondered if perhaps it had to do with the fact that he had not been on a date in some time. Yet, later, when he left to grab more boxes from his vehicle, he took an inordinately long time to walk the few feet from his apartment to the elevator doors, acutely aware of the dizzying effect the carpeting had on his senses. Sighing, he watched the elevator doors close, optimistic he would see the blonde beauty again.

Once downstairs, Megan exited the building, veering down the wide sidewalk to her shop. She turned her face briefly to the sun, relishing its warmth. The area she lived in was just a short distance from the Kennebec River. Here, there were rows of small boutiques and businesses bordering both sides of the wide road. Most of the buildings were historical, built in the Greek Revival style that had been so popular after the federal era. Megan loved that the gable ends faced forward, and most had retained their columned porches. Here and there you would see rockers of various sizes and colors, placed lovingly by the store owners for anyone to enjoy. There was a sense of community that Megan felt strongly did not exist in larger cities. The center median had beautiful red spruce as well as towering oaks that stretched their branches, forming a large canopy, sentries to the landscape surrounding them. There were bright annuals, some tiny and decorative, others loud and adventurous, representing all of the colors of the rainbow. Marigolds, with their bright yellow folds, along with snapdragons, African daisies and the fierce prophetic blue of the cornflowers, spread themselves lovingly between the small, manicured bushes. Megan observed how the rays of light danced lightly among the foliage and paused again.

Closing her eyes she raised her face, allowing the sun to kiss her gently, slowly gaining her equilibrium after the hectic morning. A vision of Brice, holding Lucy lovingly, invaded her mind and for a brief moment she felt a hot coil of desire snake its way through her body. Not one to react so strongly, she felt a moment of surprise, then quickly shrugged it off. You haven't been out on a date in a while, she reminded herself, that's all it is.

In the distance, rugged mountains rose majestically, proud and watchful as they extended themselves towards the clouds. Further down, the median ended, opening to a large sitting area with small wrought iron tables and chairs that rested on white cobblestones. A large fountain made up the center of the small plaza where she would often see shoppers casting pennies along with a wish or two into the clear water. On the weekends, different local bands would play right up to the first snow of the season, their pay only what the passing shoppers would drop into their money boxes. It was here that Megan's shop was situated.

Once a small, two-story saltbox home, Megan had converted the inside, leaving as many of the natural elements as possible. Upon entering, there was a small wooden counter to the left that faced a small table with two chairs for afternoons that were not especially busy. The upstairs held most of her larger boxes of supplies. She and Lucy loved to people watch, and Megan would most often find her eyes following the couples as they strolled by. She would wonder where they had met, or whether they were married or just dating. Sometimes she gave them names like *girl with the green hat* or *man with the flip flops* and if they appeared to be by themselves, she would try to match them up. It had occurred to her on more than one occasion that she should probably find something more useful to do with her downtime.

To the right of the door were two large glass refrigerated cases for her flowers. Shelves flanking three walls held various plants and some small gift items. Very often, Megan created one-of-a-kind arrangements and was proud of the reputation she had built. Entering the store, Megan lifted the white blinds, the same pride and excitement present as she read the bold black letters on the glass front display window, *Megan's Magnificent Stems*. Surrounding the name were stencils of lilies, her favorite flowers. Most especially, yellow lilies as they symbolized thankfulness. Megan was especially grateful for all that she had. The love of her family, Lucy, her business. She wouldn't know what to do without any of them. Bending, she took Lucy's leash off, watching fondly as she immediately ran to the back room to get into her 'work bed'. Lucy had never been a fan of exercise of any kind and although the walk was less than a half mile, with count-less sniff and pee breaks in between, she typically arrived with her tongue lolling from the side of her mouth, despite being carried the last few feet. Shaking her head, a smile playing across her lips, Megan checked her refrigerated items before heading to the back to unlock the delivery door. Her shop was usually busy but not enough to hire any help. Yet. She was ever hopeful that her business would continue to grow. Megan was still doing her own deliveries and as she opened the door, she felt relief that the delivery van was there. It was certainly not a high crime area, although, in recent weeks some of her neighbors had experi-enced the theft of their vehicles. She could use her car, but her flower arrangements could be quite large, and her economy car would never do.

Just as she was turning on her computer, her cell phone rang. Walking back to the front counter where she left it, she glanced at the caller ID. Not recognizing the number, she let it go to voicemail. Grabbing the phone, she was heading back when she heard the front door open. Megan knew before turning that her mother would be standing there, holding two cups of espresso. Like clockwork, she came every morning on her way to her secretarial job at a nearby insurance office. Even though she was happily retired, she loved to have a purpose and the fact that it was her good friend's business was a bonus. Basically, she had fun and socialized all day. Looking over her shoulder, she smiled. Elizabeth Cunningham was attired in a white sleeveless dress, small red roses adorning the hem and bodice. A red sweater, hanging off her forearm matched the ballet flats that she wore. Her short blonde hair was pulled back in a small ponytail revealing a smooth neck. Her eyes, the color of a great glass of whiskey, or so her father would always say, rested beneath feathery eyebrows above an elfin face. Her chin had a slight point that looked up to high cheekbones. Her nose was short and celestial. Greeting her, Megan grabbed one of the coffee cups as she leaned in to kiss her cheek. She smelled like lemon verbena and sunshine; a scent Megan loved. Megan looked like her mother, both the same height, five foot three. She didn't really mind being short, except maybe when it came to swimming pools. She generally had to stand on tippy toes to avoid drowning in the shallow end.

Her younger sister Lindsey, however, had inherited not only their father's dark hair and eyes, but at least some of his height. At five-foot-ten Megan was used to the attention her beautiful sister garnered wherever they went. Despite that, there was no jealousy at all between the two sisters. Theirs was a close, loving relationship and both sisters applauded each other's accomplishments. Lindsey would often say that she felt Megan was the beauty with her fair hair and petite frame. Their parents said they were both beautiful and had raised them to have confidence in themselves. Taking a sip of the rich brew, Megan watched as her mother placed her cup and purse on the counter. Just then Lucy emerged, slowly making her way to sit at Elizabeth's feet. This, too, was a daily ritual. Megan scooped Lucy up so her mother could place her customary kiss on her 'adorable squishy nose' as she so often referred to it. Laughing, Elizabeth then reached into her purse, pulling out one of Lucy's favorite treats. Lucy wiggled with excitement as she was handed the delectable morsel, then, after Megan put her down, promptly ran back to her bed to enjoy her spoils.

"Not so much as a thank you," Megan remarked, laughing as they watched the ungrateful pup trot off.

Smiling, Elizabeth took a sip of her coffee. "Well, it's lovely to have a fur grandbaby while I patiently wait for a human one," she replied, sending her daughter a wink. Sitting at one of the small chairs that flanked the front window, she draped her sweater across the seatback as she made herself comfortable.

"Ha, ha," Megan replied, leaning against the counter. "I would love to make you a grandmother but I kind of need the Prince Charming first."

Elizabeth chuckled. "Yes, yes I know," she exhaled, waving her arm. "I just wish—whoever he is—he gives up on the horse and hires an Uber. He needs to get here sooner rather than later."

Megan burst out laughing.

"Well so do I, Mom, but I'm thinking it still may be awhile."

"It will happen sweetheart, don't worry. It will happen and when it does it will be everything you ever dreamed it could be."

"Was it like that for you? I mean, I know how you and Dad met, but did you feel it? Like right away?"

Taking another sip of coffee, her mother took a moment to answer.

"I did actually," she said, a faraway look in her eyes. "It wasn't like butterflies, though," she continued, a soft expression crossing her features. "It was more like a punch in the gut."

Wide eyed, Megan suddenly remembered the new neighbor and her own heady response. Leaning her elbows on the counter, her hands cupping either side of her face, Megan waited for her mother to continue.

"'I was running late to my class, so I was in quite a hurry. Your father was standing, speaking to one of his professors. I remember, as I walked down the hall towards them, there were large windows. Just where he stood, there was a single shaft of light. When he heard my heels clicking, he turned, and our eyes met."

Spellbound, Megan thought she had never heard her mother speak like this. For a moment, she could see the shadow of the young woman she once was play softly against her features.

"What happened then?" she whispered.

"Well, I guess I must have stumbled on something because suddenly, he was by my side, his hand under my elbow to keep me from falling. When I felt his fingers touch me, I knew I would marry him. I knew it like I knew my own name. Of course, I was right," she finished, "and someday you will be right as well." Pointing towards the top of Megan's head, her expression puzzled, she asked, "Dear, why is there a feather in your hair?"

Reaching up, Megan ran her fingers over her head nervously.

"Oh, who knows?" she replied, suddenly feeling sensitive. For some reason she wasn't ready to talk about her impromptu meeting with her neighbor. Megan took the feather from her hair, smoothing it as she did so. Suddenly the door opened, an elderly woman stepping through. Casting an apologetic glance in her mother's direction, she turned to greet her customer. Checking her watch, Elizabeth gathered her things, then, throwing her daughter a kiss, she quietly left. Throughout the rest of the day Megan thought about what her mother had shared, and it solidified her own resolve to hold out for the fairy tale. Even if he comes by way of Uber, she thought, remembering the love shining from her mother's eyes, I'm holding out for the happily ever after.

That evening, Lindsey arrived for their pizza and movie night, a ritual they pinky swore would never change, no matter what. Grabbing two beers out of a bag, Lindsey handed one to Megan before putting the rest into the fridge. Truthfully, it didn't matter when Lindsey was coming over, Megan always found something she needed her to pick up on the way, so Lindsey was in the habit of dropping a quick text to let Megan know she was on her way and to see if she needed anything. Lindsey sat down by Lucy on the couch, absently stroking her head. Lucy arched her neck in response, then, deciding it was time for a belly rub, rolled onto her back, all four legs spread wide in anticipation. Sitting cross-legged in her favorite overstuffed chair, her plate of pizza resting on her lap, Megan smiled over at them. She couldn't think of anything better to do on a Friday night. There had been the usual argument over whether they would rent a horror, Megan's favorite, or a comedy, Lindsey's favorite. They had decided on a coin toss, and it looked like it would be a comedy. It was the third time in a row that Lindsey had won the toss. If it weren't for the fact that a different coin was used every time, Megan would have been convinced that her sister had rigged the whole thing. Watching her eat a fourth slice of pizza, handing Lucy small pieces in between, Megan wondered for the millionth time where she put it.

It had to be her height, she thought, as she watched Lindsey fold her long legs under her. They both had waist length hair, although, where Lindsey's was stick straight, Megan's was naturally curly. In true sister fashion each thought the other had the best hair. Tonight, both women had opted for a loose top knot. Lindsey, who was in her second year of college, had no homework, so they planned on staying up late. They ate in companionable silence and after they finished, Lindsey offered to clean up. Taking that as an opportunity, Megan checked her phone messages. A number she hadn't recognized had left a message. Listening, Megan let out a small groan.

"Is something wrong?" Lindsey asked.

With a slight shake of her head Megan replied, "No, it's just my dentist appointment reminder. I guess they must have a new number because it didn't show up on my caller ID. Anyway, it's this coming Monday," she sighed. The grimace on her face made Lindsey laugh.

"Why do you hate going to the dentist so much? I mean you have perfect, healthy teeth and you never, ever have a cavity, so I just don't get it."

"Seriously Lindsey, are there really people out there that can genuinely say they actually like going to the dentist? I mean they're in your mouth and you can't talk even though they're talking which I personally find very irritating since I cannot possibly answer them."

"They don't expect you to answer them though. It's just a kind of courtesy, to make you feel comfortable."

"But that's just it. It's not comfortable and I don't want them to talk to me. It's bad enough I'm trying to keep from swallowing whatever hellish organisms are living between my teeth as they're shooting water bullets that feel like jackhammers into my mouth, but to invite me to speak is just lunacy."

By now Lindsey was doubled over in laughter, tears running down her cheeks.

"It's not funny," Megan grumbled indignantly, joining in laughter as Lindsey's infectious humor washed over her. Grabbing a pillow from the floor, she threw it at her sister.

"Ok, Ok," Lindsey giggled, blocking the flying pillows with her arm. "Truce?"

"I'll stop IF you take Lucy for a potty break before we start our movie," Megan threatened, holding her last pillow up in the air.

"Deal," Lindsey crowed, jumping up. Grabbing her sandals, she quickly slipped them on, then, reaching for Lucy's leash, stood, waiting for Lucy to get off the couch. Stretching, Lucy looked over at Lindsey, blinking her dark eyes. Megan joined Lindsey by the door, and both women stood, tapping their feet, continuing the stare down until, inevitably, Lucy jumped down, making her way to them as slowly as she possibly could without going backwards. Arriving, she stood rigidly, resigned to her fate.

Just as they were ready to go, Megan said, "I know you keep a firm grip on her," nodding her head towards Lucy, who presently had her nose pressed against the door, her way of being passive aggressive, "but she got away from me the other day and it was a nightmare."

"She did?" Lindsey asked, surprised. Megan was a fanatic about Lucy's safety. "Outside?"

"No, it was here in the building. Actually, a new neighbor moved in two doors down and she ran into the unit while the movers were there."

"Wait. What? When were you going to tell me that bit of news?" Lindsey asked incredulously. "So, was the new resident home?"

"Oh, yes he was, but—"

"He? Your new neighbor is a 'he'? Do tell," Lindsey demanded, eyes wide with excitement.

Sighing heavily, Megan glanced down at Lucy, now lying on the floor, nose still pressed against the door.

"Yes, it's a 'he,'" Megan responded, regretting she had brought the subject up at all.

"His name is Brice something and Lucy basically introduced herself by scratching his leather couch, ripping one of his throw pillows to shreds and then, because she really wanted to make it memorable, proceeded to pee on his expensive wooden floors."

Lindsey's eyes were like saucers as she burst out laughing. "Oh no. Oh I would have given anything to have been there. Was he mad?" she chortled, in between bouts of snorts.

"He was actually very nice and very sweet. Lucy absolutely adored him which was a shocker and he really seemed to be taken with her—equally as shocking," she finished, again glancing down at Lucy who had now shifted to lying on her side, nose still pressed against the door.

By now Lindsey was staring at her sister intently. There had been something in her expression just then, in her voice as she spoke about him that piqued her curiosity.

"Is there a Mrs. Brice?" she asked.

"Well, he wasn't wearing a ring," Megan informed her sister, wincing the instant the words were out. Here it comes, she thought. I'm absolutely doomed.

"So, you noticed, which means you purposely looked, which means you thought he was cute. Did you think he was cute? What does he look like?" Lindsey was virtually hopping from one foot to the other in her excitement. Neither woman noticed that Lucy was now lying on her back, chewing her leash, her nose facing the ceiling.

Megan held up her hand. "It wasn't intentional and he's not bad looking," which Megan knew was a lie. He was a Greek God for goodness' sake, but for some reason she didn't want to share what she had felt when she met Brice. It was too new and confusing and frankly she didn't know if she would ever even see the man again, the thought of which made her stomach clench. "But right now, you really need to take Lucy out," she insisted.

Sensing that her sister was not going to reveal any further details, Lindsey grudgingly relented.

"Fine," she sighed, sliding Lucy away from the door with her foot as she opened it. "But if you meet him again, promise you will tell me?"

Smiling, Megan reached out her right hand. "I pinky swear it."

Laughing, Lindsey grasped her pinky, then gave her a quick hug. Megan watched her sister as she carried Lucy to the elevator. She had refused to walk, which she often did when she was especially angry. Lindsey was also waving her hands as she entered the elevator. That was a sure sign that Lucy had gas. Shaking her head, she couldn't stop herself from glancing down the hall towards Brice's unit. As she quietly closed the door, she told herself that she was not disappointed that Brice still had made no effort to see her again. "Well, can you blame him?" she mumbled under her breath as she made her way to sit down. Poor man was probably still trying to repair the damage from our impromptu meeting. Sighing heavily, she rested her head against the pillow, determined to put Brice Whatshisname out of her mind, once and for all.

# CHAPTER 3

Saturday dawned sunny and bright. Lindsey had plans with friends so after breakfast, she left after giving quick hugs to both Megan and Lucy. Megan would be meeting Gabby at Waterfront Park which was nearby. She hadn't seen her best friend in several weeks and was anxious to catch up on all her news. Gabby was a nurse at Mid Coast Hospital and Megan thought she was perhaps one of the most amazing women she had ever known, with an incredibly warm and generous demeanor. She had always been there to lend a hand or an ear. The two had met in college and the connection had been instant. Megan couldn't remember a time that Gabby had not been there for her, even on her honeymoon. A few days after her wedding, Megan had twisted her ankle and ended up in the emergency room. A mutual friend had texted Gabby a picture of Megan's bandaged foot. Within minutes, Megan's cell was ringing. It was Gabby, worried about her friend.

Smiling at the memory, Megan put her wayward hair in a top knot, then, donning her shorts and a t-shirt, sat on the couch to put her sneakers on. She glanced over to Lucy's bed, its occupant currently snoring. She was lying on her back, all four legs splayed wide open. The flaps of her mouth were flopped open with bits of drool running down both sides. Megan thought it was the most beautiful thing she had ever seen. Standing, she crossed the room, bending to place a soft kiss on Lucy's warm belly. Lucy stirred, slowly opening her eyes. Smiling, Megan rubbed her belly gently, and within a few moments Lucy was wide awake.

"Come on, sleepy head," she said, as she stood. Walking to the kitchen she took one last sip of coffee and placed the cup in her sink. She turned, taking Lucy's leash from the peg. Instantly, Lucy stood and after a stretch and a yawn, came to stand by Megan, waiting patiently to have her leash attached. Grabbing her backpack filled with Lucy's goodies, along with plenty of bottled water, they stepped into the hall.

She couldn't help glancing towards Brice's door, something she now did every time she either left or was coming home. She once again remembered his question about maybe meeting sometime but Megan brushed it off. "He was probably just being polite," she thought. Still, she stared at his closed door until the elevator doors opened, finally admitting to herself as she stepped in that she really was disappointed that she hadn't seen him. What is wrong with me, she asked herself, feeling suddenly frustrated. She wondered, as the elevator descended, what he was doing today. It was a Saturday, so he was probably out with his stunning supermodel girlfriend and Megan felt a strange twist in her gut at the picture it pulled up in her mind. Suddenly, the elevator stopped, and Megan realized they had only gone down three floors. As the doors opened, Megan's heart sank. It was Mrs. Milkin. For some strange reason she sensed the woman didn't like her, although Megan couldn't for the life of her figure out why. She was a short, exceedingly thin woman who stood ramrod straight, as though there were a steel bar holding her upright. Her short gray hair was brushed back, resting just below her ears. Small, deep-set eyes peered out of a pale complexion. Megan guessed her age to be approximately seventy. All her clothes were the exact same shade of black and Megan couldn't help but wonder how she had managed to match them so perfectly. When she saw Lucy, her expression, which was usually stoic, became pinched, as though she had suddenly sniffed something unpleasant. Megan pulled tightly on Lucy's leash, drawing her back protectively as Mrs. Milkin, with a brief nod in Megan's general direction, turned her back. She stood so straight that Megan could see the bones of her shoulder blades pointing against the fabric of her blouse. Hitting the lobby button again, they began their descent, the silence in the tiny space amplifying Lucy's breathing, which sounded like air being pushed in and out of a pair of bellows. Her occasional snort kept it interesting. Megan willed the elevator to move faster but it continued its slow crawl down. Suddenly, the stillness was broken by a tight, whistling sound, very similar to the air being let slowly out of a balloon. Megan's eyes widened in horror as, casting her eyes downward, she realized instantly what had just disastrously occurred. Lucy had bouts of flatulence and within seconds the smell permeated the elevator. Megan watched as the fumes reached Mrs. Milkin. Her shoulders stiffened as she raised her hand to cover her nose, then, turning her head slightly, glared at Lucy. Completely unaffected, Lucy, sat comfortably back on her haunches, gazing up at Mrs. Milkin unapologetically. Megan's eyes began to water, and she coughed as once again, the whistling sound emerged. Feeling the need to apologize she opened her mouth to speak but closed it just as quickly when Mrs. Milkin lifted her hand to silence her. Mere seconds later, the elevator doors finally opened, and the poor woman rushed out, gasping quietly for air as she wiped the tears from her eyes. Megan and Lucy stepped out after her and watched as she made her way out of the building, not once looking back. Feeling a tug on the leash, Megan looked down at Lucy who was anxious to start their adventure. Shaking her head slightly, Megan let out a chuckle. As they started forward, the chuckle turned into a laugh and by the time the two had turned the corner towards the parking lot, Megan was laughing so hard her stomach hurt. Life with Lucy was, in a word, hilarious.

Arriving at the park a short time later, Megan spotted her friend, Gabby, immediately. She was sitting at a picnic table by the swings, watching the mothers push their children, the sound of their pealing laughter rising through the treetops that bordered the amazing summit in the distance. Gabby's thick auburn hair was pulled up in a simple ponytail. When she turned, spotting Megan and Lucy approach, her startlingly pale green eyes lit with pleasure. Standing, she hugged Megan, then bent quickly to acknowledge Lucy who was trying to climb up her leg. Laughing, they all sat back down, Lucy resting at Gabby's feet. The two women quickly caught up on each other's lives and soon were laughing uproariously as they always had when they were together. Gabby had such a positive attitude towards life and found pleasure in the simple things. It was such a joy to share a friendship with her. Soon they sat in companionable silence, both just enjoying the beauty of the day and this special time together. Suddenly, Gabby reached across the table and grabbed her hand.

Her tone serious, she began. "I can't wait any longer. I have to tell someone and of course it must be you," she finished, her voice shaky. Instantly concerned, Megan responded.

"Is everything alright? You're not sick or anything are you?"

Gabby shook her head no.

"Well, I am sick," she amended, "but it's a good kind of sickness." Staring into her friend's eyes, Megan suddenly knew.

"Oh Gabby," she began, her eyes beginning to water. "Are you pregnant?" and before the words were out, Gabby was nodding yes. They both stood, Megan rushing around the picnic table. Both women hugged each other, tears of happiness sliding down their cheeks. Pulling back, Megan glanced down at Gabby's stomach. It looked the same.

Laughing, Gabby spoke. "I'm only eight weeks along so I'm not showing yet."

"I'm so very happy for you," Megan gushed, reaching out and squeezing her friend's hands. Even Lucy was excited, jumping up and down, although she couldn't possibly know why. The two friends stared into each other's eyes, recognizing how very precious this moment was. Life was going to change for both, however, Megan felt no jealousy for her friend's happiness. Instead, she was excited about the future.

"We haven't told any of our other friends," Gabby said, "just Steven's parents and of course mine, and now you. I just had to tell you even though it's very early."

"I am so glad you did," Megan said. "I can't tell you how excited I am. And nervous."

"I know," Gabby replied. "I'm scared to death, to tell you the truth. I mean, I've never been a mother, but I already love this little being so much and Steven does as well. I want you to be a part of this baby's life, so Steven and I talked about it, and we already know that we want you to be the baby's godmother. If you want to, that is?"

"Yes, of course!" Megan exclaimed. "I absolutely would love it. I am so excited," she beamed. Gabby's face softened as she observed how sincere Megan's happiness was. "We have so much to look forward to," Megan continued, "the baby shower, shopping for baby clothes, setting up the nursery..." Megan was clapping her hands gleefully. "Speaking of baby clothes, do you and Steven want to know what you're having?"

"Well, we did talk about it and decided yes, we do want to know. We both felt it would be easier in the planning of the nursery. I wanted to make sure that we had everything we needed for her or him."

"I cannot wait to find out. Please let me know if you need anything, like soup, or whatever it is pregnant women need," she finished, laughing.

"Oh, I definitely will," Gabby promised, reaching her pinky out for their pinky promise. As was always the case when the two friends were together, time had flown by, and they had to go. Gabby rose, gathering her things together, then bent down to place a kiss on Lucy's forehead.

The two women walked to their cars together, stopping only once so Megan could pick Lucy up. She had decided that walking was out of the question and had suddenly stopped, flipping onto her back, her tongue hanging out of the side of her mouth, doing her best impression of a corpse. Megan presumed this was for effect. After a final brief hug, the two friends promised to be in touch soon and Megan was on her way back home. Lucy was fast asleep in the back seat, exhausted from a day that had consisted of no exercise whatsoever. Tomorrow was Sunday and Megan looked forward to a quiet day at home. There was a new recipe for dog treats she wanted to try, and very possibly there would be an old movie classic happening as well. Smiling, Megan felt a moment of intense gratitude for all that she had. Life is good, she thought. Maybe not as exciting as she would like, but good, nonetheless.

It was only an hour later that Megan's heart sank as she walked into her home and remembered she had a dental appointment the next morning. Ugh! Oh well, she thought, as she got ready to shower. With the sun, a little rain must fall. Little did she know, it wouldn't be a little rain coming her way. It was going to be a monsoon.

---

Since Lindsey had no classes on Monday, she offered to watch the shop all day while Megan went to her dental appointment.

Loving the idea of a three-day weekend, Megan had accepted happily. She had been seeing Dr. Kilbran since the age of thirteen and had grown very fond of him. Occasionally he would pop into the store and grab some fresh flowers for his wife of forty years. "Just because," he would say, with a wink in her direction. Megan thought it was just about the most romantic thing ever and it made her suddenly realize it had been several months since he had been in the shop.

Megan pulled into a parking spot in front of the building, located in a small strip plaza with a salon, sandwich shop and dog grooming facility. Like most doctors Dr. Kilbran had joined up with several other dentists when costs became too high for him to remain solo, however, he had assured her she could continue to see him. With a quick glance in her rear-view mirror, Megan got out of her car, adjusting her t-shirt over her favorite pair of ripped jeans. As she did so, it occurred to her that she should have maybe put on a bit of makeup but then, it's just Dr. Kilbran she thought, and this is a 'me' day.

Her mass of hair was piled on her head in a haphazard top knot that kept falling to the side because of the weight. Just as she entered the building, Megan reached up, tightening the elastic. The woman behind the counter looked over when she stepped in. Megan realized this was a new receptionist. Older, her charcoal hair was highlighted by streaks of silver. Megan thought she was stunning but wondered what had happened to his old secretary. Moving forward, she signed in on the sheet as the receptionist, whose nametag read Peggy, greeted her.

"How are you today?" she asked, smiling widely.

"Well, I guess as good as I can be, visiting the dentist," Megan joked nervously as the secretary handed her some information to fill out. "Thankfully Dr. Kilbran knows just how to ease my jitters," she continued, turning to search for an empty seat in the busy waiting room.

"Oh wait," Peggy began, looking down at the sign in sheet. "I'm afraid Dr. Kilbran is no longer here. He retired several months ago. You will be seeing Dr. Castillo," she continued. "He has been with us for three weeks. I think you will really like him."

Megan's heart sank as she tried to hide how badly the news that her favorite doctor was no longer here was affecting her. Also, she couldn't place it, but she was positive she had heard that name somewhere else recently.

"Oh, ok," Megan replied, a sinking sensation in the pit of her stomach. Turning again, she found a seat, quickly filling out her paperwork. After returning it, she sat, crossing her legs, her left foot moving back and forth nervously. It wasn't fear really, just some jitters. Megan hated dental work of any kind. Not that she had had much but she did have to have an extraction once and while she hadn't been in any pain, the process itself had been nerve wracking. She had fallen off her bicycle and her tooth had sustained trauma. As a result, it could not be saved. Since then, she had maintained perfect dental visits with no cavities ever found. There is no reason to believe this visit will be any different, she told herself. It's just a new doctor and maybe I will like him just as much as Dr. Kilbran although, at the thought, Megan mentally shook her head. Pulling her phone out of her purse, she checked for messages. Lindsey had Lucy today as well, so Megan wanted to be sure there had been no emergencies, which, whenever Lucy was around, seemed to occur quite frequently. Seeing there were none, she replaced her phone. Just as she was zipping her purse her name was called. Standing, she walked towards the smiling dental assistant, feeling a bit like she was headed to the gallows.

She was ushered into an exam room, and after hanging her purse on a hook by the door, Megan made herself as comfortable as possible in the dental chair. Glancing at her feet, which were visible in her white flip flops, she briefly regretted having put off her pedicure until next week. The assistant was very pleasant and after asking Megan a few more questions, advised her the doctor would be in shortly. Nodding in her general direction, Megan heard the door close quietly behind her and settled back to wait. Looking around the small room, she noticed that they had painted the walls a glorious turquoise blue color. Megan remembered the dismal brown it used to be, and mentally thanked whoever was responsible for the new color choice. There really wasn't too much else in the room to occupy her mind except the small machine to her left. It was a type of sink with two clear tubes coming from one end. Megan assumed it was where you rinsed and spit. Glancing over her shoulder at the still closed door she quickly reached over. Picking up the first tube, she observed a small red button close to the end. Curious to know what it did she pointed it away from herself towards her feet. Instantly, she could hear the sucking sound and knew it went inside your mouth to get rid of the excess water when they were cleaning or doing other procedures. She placed the tube back and picked up the second one. It too had a small button but this one was a bright blue. Wondering why it was a different color, she pressed the button, forgetting to point it away. Instead, it was pointed directly at her face. The surprisingly strong water stream hit Megan just below her eye. In her panic, she waved it away towards the door. That was the moment her new dentist stepped in, his greeting dying as the water hit him directly on the forehead. Reacting quickly, he turned so that the remaining water hit him behind his ear. Megan was so completely horrified that for the first few moments it took for her to return the tube to its proper resting place, all while apologizing profusely, she never even looked at the poor man. Quickly wiping the rest of her dripping face, she turned slightly as he walked fully into the room, facing her directly. Oh no, Megan thought. No, no, no.

Closing her eyes briefly, she felt the heat of her embarrassment so acutely, that droplets of sweat formed immediately on her forehead, climbing from her neck to her face. No, this cannot, absolutely cannot be happening, she cried inwardly. But, she knew, without a doubt, that it most assuredly was, indeed, happening. Standing directly in front of her, still patting the water from his face and hair was Brice. Beautiful, tall, better looking than she remembered, Brice. Her new dentist.

# CHAPTER 4

*M*egan could see his eyes widen in surprise when he recognized her. Chuckling, he reached out to shake her hand. "Why is it that when you and I are in the same room, some small disaster happens?"

Smiling nervously, all Megan could do was shake her head, the ability to converse normally having left her. Why does that keep happening, she wondered, beginning to think that she might have some weird medical issue. Finally, mustering together what little dignity was left after their last encounter, she answered.

"I wish I could blame this one on Lucy but I'm afraid this was all me." Pointing to the sink, she continued, "I guess I may have been a bit too curious, and water happened," she finished, shrugging. "I really am sorry."

"No need to be sorry," he replied, laughter in his eyes. "I happen to be fond of small disasters now and then especially," he continued, pulling a small chair over and sitting, "when it involves a certain beauty..." Megan's eyes widened, her heart suddenly beating furiously, "who likes ripping my pillows and peeing on my floors," he finished, smiling brilliantly.

Realizing he had been referring to Lucy, Megan felt a quick stab of disappointment.

With a small laugh, Megan found herself staring into Brice's eyes. That blue though, she thought. A girl could get lost in those eyes. Realizing she was staring; Megan was again embarrassed. He smelled wonderful and she couldn't help but notice that beneath his jacket, his dark pants were molded to his thighs. It took everything she had not to reach over and run her fingers along their length. The thought sent a slice of excitement throughout her body. Squirming, she tried to ignore the sensation. Megan had never felt this level of sexual tension. It was palpable.

Suddenly, she realized that Brice was staring at her just as intently. In that moment, Megan knew he felt the attraction just as strongly as she did. The room was replete with their mutual desire. Abruptly, Brice pushed back his chair and stood. Seeming to shake himself free of the intense exchange, he became immediately businesslike. It was a relief, as Megan was overwhelmed by the sheer force of her attraction to this man.

The appointment was a blur, but when he had been leaning over her examining her teeth, she had become fixated on the pulse in his neck. She imagined herself running her tongue lightly over it and could almost taste the slight saltiness of his skin.

Finally, it was over. Her teeth were healthy. Thankfully, all she would need would be a cleaning, which she planned on scheduling when she checked out. Brice helped her from her chair and Megan was surprised to find that her legs were particularly shaky. Just the feel of his hand on her arm caused her breasts to tighten, her breathing to become rapid. It was like nothing she had ever experienced. Suddenly, Megan wanted to escape. There was too much happening at once. When she was this close to him, she could feel her control slipping. She wasn't sure if perhaps she had just imagined his interest, as his demeanor now was wholly professional. Megan shook his hand, something she was getting used to, and bolted out of the office. Once she had scheduled her cleaning, which would not be with Brice, thank goodness, she couldn't get home fast enough. She needed to digest everything that she was feeling, which was almost exclusively sexual frustration and confusion. Megan was grateful that she had projects at home to occupy her, although, deep down, she knew Brice would never be far from her thoughts.

Exiting the elevator, Brice turned towards his apartment but not before he stopped twice, once to be sure he had his house key and once to be sure he had remembered his wallet. He kept glancing surreptitiously at Megan's door and found himself disappointed when he didn't see her. And Lucy. For some crazy reason he liked her destructive dog almost as much as he did Megan. Stepping into his softly lit apartment, he tossed his jacket onto the easy chair next to the couch. As Brice crossed the room, he slid his shoes off, unbuttoning the top four buttons of his shirt as he made his way to the refrigerator. Relieved to see he wasn't out of beer; he retrieved the cold brew then headed back to the living room. Brice leaned back into the couch with a sigh, propping his feet on the coffee table. Gulping deeply, he swallowed, then, closing his eyes, let himself sink into the soft leather.

He was still adjusting to his new surroundings and to a whole new set of patients, most of whom had sung the praises of his predecessor Dr. Kilbran their entire visit. Leaning forward, he took another long swallow and glancing down saw a small scratch in the leather cushion. Lucy. Instantly, he thought of Megan and his body responded, blood rushing to his nether regions. Shaking his head, he tried to dismiss the image of her from his mind. It had been a week since he had seen her in his office, and this was still happening. He was no schoolboy and could not understand this forceful attraction to her. To the thought of her. Brice found her not necessarily beautiful in the conventional sense, yet he couldn't help but notice how clear her skin had been, devoid of any makeup and with the tiny freckles along the bridge of her nose. Her complexion was nearly flawless, with a slight natural pout to lips that while not overly full, had an unusually deep pink color. Brice had found her instantly entrancing. Around her he had felt his restraint slipping. A man who had always known exactly what he wanted; Brice had made it happen. He had done that by being in control. Every aspect of his life had been planned out, starting in his junior year of high school and continuing through college and then dental school. Brice had worked hard but it had all been worth it. Now, at just thirty-three, he felt as though he had finally achieved his goals.

Moving to Maine from Orlando had been a good decision as he was ready to take on more patient responsibility but preferred a more intimate setting. Here he woke each day to a rugged vista that soothed his soul. He also loved skiing and was looking forward to his first winter. His parents were divorced, his mother, Olivia living in Ontario and his father, Tony in California. His sister, Amy was still in Orlando, working as an entertainment manager for a large hotel chain. It was just the two of them, so they were especially close, although they did have a large extended family.

Their Cuban heritage assured lively family gatherings and of course, extraordinary food. Amy had lamented his move, worried that they would lose touch, although she too loved the idea of learning to ski as her brother had. Brice had assured both his sister and mother that they would see each other often and he meant to keep that promise.

Family was especially important to him, more so since the divorce of his parents after almost forty years of marriage. Neither he nor Amy had ever seen anything to indicate that their parents' marriage was suffering. In the end, Olivia and Tony had sat their grown children down to share the truth of their relationship. Both his mother and father had realized that while they had a deep regard and respect for each other, they long ago had stopped being in love. Brice could not understand how it was possible to fall out of love and was so relentless in his questioning that his parents had finally acquiesced, admitting that they had not married for love. His mother had been pregnant with him, and they had made the decision to marry. It had all been shocking at the time, however now they were all living the lives they were meant to. His mother ran a clothing boutique, small but doing well. His father was living his dream in Napa Valley where he opened his own optometry office and a month ago had remarried a wonderful woman who he was most assuredly deeply in love with. They had all attended the simple ceremony, even their mother, her own fiancé in attendance as well. Amy and Brice had given their father away. It had been an emotional time for them all, as well as a profoundly healing time.

Now Brice looked forward to growing his career and perhaps meeting that special woman, although his plan did not include marriage for a very long time. He was enjoying the fruits of his labors too much. Freedom from studying and exams and making up for missed parties and especially missed fun. Brice was ready to see exactly what Maine had to offer and would be starting this Friday night. He and a few of his co-workers were making a night of it and he hoped beautiful women would be involved. At the thought, however, Brice was suddenly struck with a feeling of guilt, an image of Megan suddenly at the forefront of his thinking. It almost felt as though he were cheating on her. Shaking his head at the ridiculous thought, Brice quickly showered, changing into a comfortable pair of shorts and a polo. He turned on the television, clicking through various channels, but could find nothing he was interested in watching.

His thoughts once again turned to Megan and with a frustrated groan he stood, pacing the room. More than anything

Brice wanted to walk down to her apartment and ask her out. He was convinced that this was all just in his head or possibly somewhere else. Still, as he walked towards the door, he hesitated. There was something about how Megan made him feel that unsettled him. It was true, he realized. He was afraid to ask her out. The entire time she had been in his office he had found himself practicing a way to ask her out that didn't sound like he was still a schoolboy, or worse, desperate. None of this behavior was familiar to him and he wasn't sure he wanted to pursue it. With that thought, he sat down heavily, running his hands impatiently through his dark hair.

Settling back once again, he grabbed his cell phone. He would call Amy and see if maybe she would like to come for the weekend. He had a ton of points so the airline tickets would cost virtually nothing. A distraction is just what he needed to get Megan and Lucy out of his mind. He couldn't help smiling to himself as he remembered the chaos that little dog had wrought in just a few short minutes. After a brief conversation, Amy agreed to come on Saturday. Brice was relieved that surely these restless thoughts regarding Megan would go away. He was positive they would and leaning on his belief that this was an anomaly, and he could certainly control himself around Megan should they happen to meet again, Brice finally relaxed, settling into a football game. In no time at all he would probably not even remember her name.

Amy arrived at exactly eleven a.m. on Saturday, rushing towards him through the airport terminal at breakneck speed, she launched her five-foot frame into his arms, covering his cheeks with kisses. Her long black hair, echoing his own, ended just at the small of her back. Unlike Brice's ice blue eyes, Amy's were as dark as her hair, giving her an exotic look. Petite but curvy, Brice was used to the attention his beautiful sister garnered and often some unlucky man was the recipient of his angry glare. They had always been overly protective of one another, and Brice would have it no other way. They had planned on walking downtown to explore the shops and maybe have lunch. Brice had still not had a chance to explore his surroundings, so he was looking forward to their outing. The previous evening spent with friends out on the town had left Brice feeling flat. While fun, he felt there was something missing. It wasn't anything Brice could put his finger on, although he had found himself wondering what Megan did with her time off. He didn't believe she was married as he had taken several opportunities to see if there was a tell-tale ring present. Having observed none, he felt sure she was single. Of course, he knew that did not necessarily mean that she was free and immediately tried to dispel knot the sudden spark of jealousy the thought elicited.

Since Amy had never been to his new home, Brice gave her a quick tour, dropping her luggage into the spare room. After she freshened up, they were on their way. Walking towards the elevator Brice could not help but glance towards Megan's door. He couldn't tell if he was relieved or disappointed when he didn't see her, though he suspected it was a little of both. Amy chatted all the way down and was practically running by the time they made it to the sidewalk. Brice could hear music in the distance and as they approached the shops, he could see a small band playing alongside a large fountain. There were people everywhere, the sounds of children's happy screams and laughter filling the air.

Brice instantly felt at home. Large crowds and music reminded him of his childhood and all the parties his parents had held in their home. Everyone would bring a dish, but his favorite had always been his grandmother Fela's rice and beans. The undisputed matriarch of the family, she and his grandfather Antonio, Tony as everyone called him, immigrated to America, providing a wealth of love and wisdom throughout his life. They were both gone now, and Brice still felt their absence keenly, especially when he needed advice. Somehow, Fela had always been able to steer him on the right path and he credited much of his success to them both, as well as to the sacrifices his own parents had made.

Brice suddenly felt a rush of gratitude envelop him and, glancing down at his sister clapping and tapping her feet to the music, he suddenly laughed. Grabbing her hand, he began a salsa dance. With an excited scream, she jumped right in. Soon, children and adults alike joined them. It was more fun than he had had in a long time. It felt good to finally be on this side of his goals. They danced their way around the fountain until finally, breathless, they took a break. Brice was scoping out a place to eat when suddenly, his eye caught sight of a dog. A very familiar dog, that was currently racing towards him like a small black cannonball. Eyes widening, Brice put his arms out to try to stop what he already sensed was about to happen. The dog ran straight at him, then leapt, landing squarely on his chest. Holding the animal securely against him, Brice fell backwards into the fountain. His long legs draped over the concrete ledge while from his back to his head, he was covered in water. Since the fountain was not deep, the water did not cover him completely. Stunned, he lay there for a moment until he felt the creature wriggling in his grasp. Loosening his grip, the dog's head came up. Lucy. Her slightly wet muzzle dripped onto his cheek as she looked down at him, her mischievous eyes blinking rapidly, her tongue lolling out one side of her mouth. Brice watched in fascination as a small stream of drool landed on his favorite polo. He was aware of people rushing towards him, some with concern and others whose guffaws of laughter he could hear and did not appreciate. Even Amy looked as though she were trying desperately not to laugh. Then, just as he was finally able to sit up, still holding the wriggling body closely, it occurred to him that where there was Lucy there would be Megan.

As if thinking her into being, she was suddenly standing in front of him, her expression of horror almost comical as she rushed forward to help. Reaching in, she grabbed Lucy, hauling her off Brice's chest. As he stood, he realized that despite what had just happened, despite his drool sodden clothes, sore back and abject embarrassment, he could not stop grinning. It was at that very moment, as his heart rate accelerated just seeing Megan, that Brice knew, without a doubt, that he was in big trouble. The biggest trouble ever.

Megan had reached an entirely new level of humiliation. Brice was soaked, his clothes ruined, and it was all her fault. If she had not been spying so intently on him and his stunning companion through her shop window, she would have realized that a customer had left the door open just wide enough for Lucy to slip out unnoticed. Megan had been so involved that it wasn't until she observed Lucy running towards Brice that she had even realized she was loose. Now, not only would he think she was an absolute dimwit, but she would also have the great pleasure of meeting his partner under less than stellar circumstances. Feeling Lucy struggling, she placed her down, bending as she did so to clip on her leash. Standing, she looked down at the front of her brand-new silk blouse. Wet. It was her favorite, as well as her most expensive garment. Mentally, she was screaming, while outwardly, she was trying to regain some composure. Since the day that Lucy entered her world, Megan had realized that her superpower was the ability to lose her mind and remain calm simultaneously. However, even her superpower hadn't saved her from the despair that had washed over her when she had spotted Brice dancing with his gorgeous companion. It felt as though she had been kicked in the stomach which was followed closely with an acute flash of jealousy.

Now, as she watched the brunette beauty help Brice out of the fountain, she understood completely. I mean, look at him, she thought, observing the way his now wet polo stuck to every muscle on his stomach, each one clearly defined. Did the man have any fat? she wondered. Then, as he turned, bending to retrieve his wallet, Megan was gifted with yet another visual, eliciting an inward groan. She tried to appear contrite as Brice walked towards her, the beauty by his side.

As soon as he was close enough, Brice bent, giving Lucy, who was straining to get to him, a quick rub on her wet head. Standing, his gaze brushed over Megan intently, his blue eyes running quickly over her body. A rush of heat washed over her, along with a swift physical reaction that was almost agonizing. However, her mind was at war with her body.

"Well, we meet again," Brice said, clearly amused. Pointing to Lucy, he continued. "We may need to put a warning label on her soon if this keeps up." The young woman beside him laughed, her hand coming to rest on his bulging forearm. Megan inwardly flinched. She clearly loved him and here he was, being completely inappropriate with those eyes of his, making her feel things she had no business feeling.

"Yes, well I apologize yet again," Megan replied, her tone cool. "I insist you let me reimburse you for the damages."

A puzzled expression crossed Brice's features.

"It's not necessary," he began but Megan quickly interrupted.

"No, it is necessary," she replied, spitting out the words. "Lucy has done this twice and it was my fault since I wasn't paying attention."

Amy, observing the exchange, was perplexed.

"Well, I'm not going to accept any reimbursement," Brice responded firmly, finding himself suddenly at odds with her attitude.

Ignoring his statement and refusing to meet his eyes, Megan continued. "I will drop a check at your home this afternoon."

Brice's jaw clenched as he stepped closer to Megan.

"I will not cash it," he whispered harshly, "a check?" he repeated, his voice dripping with sarcasm. "Do they still make those?"

By now Amy's head was snapping back and forth like a slingshot. A gentle smile lighting her face, she stepped forward.

"Brice, you haven't introduced us," she stated, offering Megan a level but friendly stare. "Obviously the two of you or," here she smiled down at Lucy, "should I say the three of you have met so I'm afraid I am at a complete disadvantage."

Startled, both Megan and Brice turned their attention to Amy. So intent had they been during their heated exchange, they had forgotten her entirely.

Embarrassed, Brice apologized.

"I'm sorry, yes of course. Amy, this is Megan, my neighbor. We met the day I moved in, and this beauty," he continued, nodding towards Lucy, "is the mischievous pooch who introduced us."

Amy held out her hand warmly.

"So nice to meet you, Megan," she said. "Sometimes my brother can forget his manners," she continued, her dark eyes dancing with merriment.

"Brother?" Megan squeaked, quickly clearing her throat. "You're his sister," she continued, a giant smile suddenly lighting her face. "Oh! I thought, well, it doesn't matter," Megan continued, pumping Amy's hand up and down enthusiastically. "Yes, I can see the resemblance." Suddenly, realizing she was rambling, she dropped Amy's hand and quickly stepped back.

---

Brice, who had been watching the exchange, was utterly confused. One minute Megan had appeared angry and now she was smiling happily, as though nothing had ever happened.

Shaking his head slightly, Brice chalked it up to the fact that he wasn't that great at understanding women. Clearly. Pulling on her leash, Lucy, who had been sitting quietly during the exchange, was trying to climb up Brice. With a chuckle he bent down as Lucy scrambled onto his muscular leg, craning her neck to deposit her signature sloppy kisses onto his willing cheek. He found himself somewhat grateful for the distraction that Lucy afforded him. It appeared as though every time he was in near proximity to Megan, he found himself off balance. It was an unfamiliar and surprising observation. Brice was also cognizant that Megan's approval mattered to him. Glancing up he observed her easy camaraderie with his sister and something else stirred within his chest. He watched as she laughed at something Amy said while impatiently brushing a stray piece of hair out of her eyes. Sighing heavily, he admitted the truth to himself. While he wasn't entirely sure what it was that pulled him so inexorably towards Megan, he knew that it was strong. It was something he would need to examine closely and soon.

---

Megan watched Amy glance over her shoulder towards her brother, then back, and then suggest they all have lunch together. Laughing, Brice looked down at his soaked clothes.

"Well, I think I need to change first, and poor Megan does as well I believe."

"Actually, yes, I do," Megan responded, "but I'm afraid lunch is out," she continued, disappointment clear in her voice. "I have a store here and I have to reopen soon."

"Really, what store?" Amy asked.

Turning slightly, Megan pointed to her storefront window.

"*Megan's Magnificent Stems*?" Brice stated. "You own it?" he asked, seemingly impressed.

"I sure do," Megan responded proudly.

"Well, I for one love flowers," Amy announced, "so I will definitely be by before I leave to grab something nice for Brice's man cave," she continued, casting Brice an affectionate smile. "I think calla lilies would be perfect."

"Oh, I have some gorgeous ones," Megan responded excitedly. The two women fell into step as they headed towards their respective homes to change, Lucy trotting happily ahead. Megan was aware of Brice's eyes as he followed behind. Having observed his loving treatment of Lucy had furthered her attraction to Brice resulting in a surge of emotions she was desperate to understand. Her insides felt fluttery and nervous, but in a way that excited her. It was a new feeling, foreign but wholly specific to Brice.

Just then Lucy stopped. Turning, her expressive eyes met Megan's and she could have sworn that Lucy winked. It caught her completely off guard and she shook her head slightly, not quite trusting her senses, as her canine swung her head back and continued onward. Amy asked if everything was alright. Noting her confused expression, she nodded. "I'm fine," Megan replied, convinced her eyes had played tricks on her. But all the same, a part of her wondered exactly what her faithful dog was up to.

# CHAPTER 5

*D*uring the walk home they had all exchanged phone numbers and Megan tried to control the plethora of butterflies winging around in her stomach. They had both wanted her to join them for dinner that evening, however, Megan had made plans for dinner with her parents, and she knew her mother would have already been well into the cooking stages by now. Still, she found herself hoping that Brice called her soon. There was something about this man that drew her to him, and Megan really wanted to know who he really was. Bidding them goodbye, Megan watched surreptitiously as Amy and Brice made their way to Brice's apartment, smiling at the loud swish swish of Brice's wet shoes as they made their way down the hall. As soon as Megan opened her door, Lucy rushed in, immediately making her way to her bed, curling up for a nap. Laughing, Megan went to change clothes knowing that getting Lucy back out again would be a major feat. Still, Megan couldn't help but think it had all been worth it, recollecting how Brice looked, wet. Oh yes, she thought, definitely worth it.

. . .

A week went by, and Megan still hadn't heard from Brice. This was bothering her, and she was frustrated by her attraction to him. It had occurred to her several times that her behavior was unusual. She had never responded this way to anyone, not even long-term boyfriends she thought, reminiscing about her past relationships. Always confident, she suddenly began to have feelings of doubt. What if he just doesn't want to date right now? Or maybe he just doesn't want to date me.

Standing before her full-length mirror one morning, she eyed herself critically, something she had not done since her awkward high school years. She examined her body starting from top to bottom. Your face is average, she reflected, and the riotous, out of control hair isn't going anywhere she mourned, grabbing a handful, then letting it fall back down. The breasts are fine, she thought, although, to her mind, overly large for her short stature. Turning her legs from side to side she noted they were not slim, rather, they were somewhat thick and muscular. The smallest part of her body was her waist. Sighing heavily, she turned away, throwing herself backwards onto the bed. Megan, stop, she chastised herself. If it is meant to be then it will happen. Thankfully she had received an invitation to go to a party at Gabby's, which she accepted with alacrity. Maybe this would help get her mind off Brice, she thought hopefully.

By Friday night, Megan was ready. The work week, while busy and great for business, had also been long. Megan found herself staring at Brice's door every time she stepped off the elevator, willing him to walk out so that she could at least see him. There had been countless times that she had had to stop herself from walking to his door and asking him out. Shaking her head at the thought, she knew she wouldn't. If she were honest, she was just an old-fashioned girl and she wanted him to make the first move. She knew pride had a part to play as well. A distraction in the form of a party was exactly what she needed.

After taking a long shower, Megan opted to leave her hair

down. She chose a one-piece shorts outfit that was fitted at the chest. Generally, she preferred a looser fit, but she had fallen in love with the print, deciding on impulse to buy it. A pair of high wedge sandals completed the look. She even applied makeup, a rare occurrence. Standing in front of her mirror, Megan twirled back and forth happy with the overall result. Grabbing her purse off the bed, she headed to the kitchen.

Lucy was sprawled on the couch, her favorite blanket beneath her. Her head hung partially off the edge, all four paws pointing towards the ceiling. Laughing, Megan walked over to her. Bending, she planted a kiss on her forehead then added a few raspberries to her pink belly. "Try not to burn the place down while I'm gone," Megan quipped, glancing down to be sure she had enough food and water. Satisfied that she would be comfortable, Megan reached for the door, the sound of Lucy belching following her out. Megan's eyes immediately glanced down the hall towards Brice's unit. Suddenly, she froze.

Brice was opening his door; except he was not alone. He was most emphatically not alone. A young woman was laughing up at him. She was standing on her tippy toes, whispering something in his ear. She was exquisite. He was beautiful. It was then that he saw her. His eyes widened briefly, a lopsided grin lighting his face.

Lifting his hand in a wave, Megan suddenly panicked. He's on a date she realized, her spirits plummeting. Perfect timing as usual, she told herself, slamming the button on the elevator furiously. Relief washed over her when the doors immediately opened. She could hear Brice calling her name, but she refused to answer his greeting. The elevator started down and Megan felt everything in her wilt. Slumping against the wall, she briefly closed her eyes. Suddenly Megan was furious.

"Well, that was an eye opener," she said out loud. Her voice reverberated off the walls of the elevator. What an idiot I am, she thought angrily. As the doors opened, Megan rushed out, desperately in need of fresh air. Although it was summer, the evenings were cool, and Megan relished the feel of the crisp air on her burning face. She had opted for an Uber and realized the car was already there. Getting in quickly, she gave the driver Gabby's address and was soon walking through the front door. Megan felt numb, not yet ready to talk about it with her friend.

There was a great buffet set up on the dining room table, but Megan wasn't hungry. Instead, she grabbed a cold beer as she made her way out onto the covered lanai. Some of the people were mutual friends and some Megan was meeting for the first time. It was a lively party although, feeling decidedly sorry for herself, Megan couldn't help the sudden stab of envy when she witnessed the abject love between Steven and Gabby. Had she misread Brice's interest in her? she wondered, once again picturing him and the gorgeous stranger preparing to enter his apartment.

Sensing something wasn't quite right with her friend, Gabby made her way over, sitting across from Megan. Leaning forward, her glass of apple juice resting in her cupped hands she spoke, determination in her voice.

"Alright, spill it."

"Spill what?" Megan asked, innocently. Taking a large gulp of her beer, she sat back, attempting to appear composed.

"I know you. This is not you. I have never seen you so sad. Come on," she entreated. "You'll feel better if you get it off your chest, I promise."

Sighing heavily, Megan shared her discovery that Brice clearly had a girlfriend and that she was furious that he had flirted so outrageously with her, even getting her number. "He is a terrible subhuman and a liar," she wailed. "I'm positive I will never be married or have children, although I didn't even know I wanted that until just recently." Closing her eyes, she whispered, "What in the world is wrong with me?"

Trying to hide her smile, Gabby spoke.

"So, you saw him with a woman. Do you know who she was?"

Startled, Megan's expression became thoughtful.

"Well, no," she replied, "but he was walking into his home with a woman, who, by the way, looked as though she had just arrived from her modeling job in St Moritz."

Unable to hold back, Gabby laughed loudly.

"You are incredible, do you know that? I have never heard you describe another woman, no matter the age, as anything other than beautiful, which by the way, is one the many things I love most about you. However," she continued, her concern evident, "what I'm not familiar with is the Megan who jumps to conclusions without affording the other party a chance at an explanation."

"But I saw—"

"You saw Brice laughing outside of his home with a woman you do not know. That is all. Not only that, but you said yourself that he smiled when he saw you and even though you were rude—"

"I wasn't ru—"

Holding up her hand to silence her, Gabby continued.

"Despite the fact that you were rude and ignored him, he still walked down that hall to the elevator to again try to speak to you. Now, I'm no expert, Megan, but that does not sound like a man with anything to hide."

Megan immediately felt contrite. Gabby was right. She really didn't know who the woman was or what Brice was doing, and truth be told she suddenly realized it didn't matter. They hadn't even been on a date for crying out loud. Ugh!

"You're right," Megan admitted. "Have I told you how much I appreciate all of your amazing wisdom?"

"Actually no, you have not," Gabby responded, smiling widely. "But please feel free to tell me how perfect I am. I'm all ears."

The rest of the evening was much more pleasant, and Megan had a wonderful time. She was unable to get an Uber so Mark, the husband of one of Gabby's co-workers, offered to drive Megan to her home. He and his wife Carla were expecting their second child so she had opted to stay behind so she and Gabby could talk babies.

As it turned out, Mark also wanted to talk about his babies. All the way home, he regaled Megan with stories of his first born as well as how his wife was handling her current pregnancy. Megan thought it was truly wonderful how committed he was to his family and his pride was obvious. Despite reassuring Mark she could make her way up alone, he insisted on riding up with her and seeing her to her door.

"It's late," he stated. "I would want someone to see my wife or daughter safely to their door."

Stepping off the elevator, Megan opened her door partway. Turning quickly to thank Mark, she suddenly felt her ankle twist painfully. Not used to wearing any kind of heel, she had turned the wrong way. Instinctively, Mark caught her as she began to fall. The next few moments were absolute mayhem.

As Mark reached out to catch her, the elevator doors also opened and Brice stepped out, and Lucy came crashing out of the open apartment door, barking furiously at Mark. Grabbing onto Mark to regain her balance, Megan heard a tear and realized it was Mark's shirt. Brice stood paralyzed for just a moment, then, a look of fury crossing his features, he lifted Mark off Megan, shoving him hard against the wall. Startled, Mark lost his balance, sliding down onto the floor, affording Lucy an opportunity to spring onto his chest where she proceeded to growl fiercely, a decidedly dramatic move, Megan thought, amid the fray.

Stunned, she watched the entire scene unfold, wondering when, exactly, she had lost complete control of her life. Rushing over, she scooped Lucy into her arms, carrying her back to the apartment. Placing her firmly inside, she closed the door quickly. Making her way over to Mark, she helped him as he tried to stand all while shooting daggers at Brice, who stood, like an avenging superhero, legs apart, arms folded on his chest. His expression could only be described as murderous.

"What is wrong with you?" Megan spit out furiously. "You could have killed him!"

"Well, at least you are home safely. And you're welcome," Brice replied icily. "It's not every evening you see a woman being accosted." Here, he turned his rage filled eyes towards Mark.

"Wait, what?" Mark stammered. "I most certainly was not doing any such thing!" he denied, vehemently shaking his head. Looking around for the missing piece of his sleeve, he retrieved it. Stepping past Brice nervously, he began hitting the elevator button furiously. That button is never going to survive, Megan thought.

"My mistake," Brice bit out, turning his full attention to Megan. "It must have been something else," he finished, leaving no doubt in Megan's mind as to what he meant.

Megan was beside herself, aware that she hadn't had the wherewithal to thank Mark. I will have to call and apologize to that poor man, she thought, fury and humiliation at war inside her trembling body. Turning her attention once again to Brice, she found herself barely able to speak.

"Well?" she bit out.

"Well, what?" Brice responded, his tone clipped.

"You attacked an innocent man, and you ask what? Have you lost all of your mind?"

"I stepped off the elevator and see a strange man with his hands all over your body and you're wondering why I intervened. How was I supposed to know he was your date?"

"Hands all over— They were most certainly not all over my— me," she sputtered. "Just absolutely they were not!"

"Looked like they were to me!"

"Well, they were not!"

"Then why—"

"I fell off these stupid shoes!" she yelled, reaching down and pulling off one, then the other. Limping, she approached him, holding the shoes out. "I never wear heels and I wore them tonight and I twisted my ankle and he caught me. Get it?"

Turning, she began to hobble to her door.

"You're one to talk," by the way, she bit out. "What about you and your St. Moritz model date person? She was practically licking your ear off which, I can assure you, is unsanitary. I know. My friend is a nurse."

"Wait, you're hurt," Brice interrupted, his concern evident.

"I'm fine," she said, waving her hand backwards. "Please just go."

Megan felt his arms come around her and before she knew what was happening, he was lifting her. Reflexively, she wrapped her arms around his neck. Bending slightly, he opened the door. Lucy looked anxiously upwards at Brice. He quietly whispered, "I have her, girl. Don't worry, I'll take good care of her." As if he had been there a million times, he walked quickly to her bedroom, then, laying her down gently, began to examine her foot. Sitting on the edge of the bed, he carefully lifted the injured ankle which was already slightly swollen. Megan winced slightly, but the discomfort from her ankle in no way compared to what having Brice sitting on her bed was doing to the rest of her body. Every part of her felt heightened. Fascinated, she watched his hands as they moved her ankle cautiously. Looking up, Brice caught her expression and Megan instantly observed the passion flare in his eyes.

"That woman you saw me with was my co-worker's wife. He was in my apartment. He thought we were having a guys' night, but she surprised him with a trip for their anniversary. Oh, and she isn't a model in St. Moritz, although she could be," he continued. "She teaches elementary school."

Without breaking eye contact his hand began to move slowly up her leg. In its wake, her skin burned as the heat began to climb higher. Her nipples tightened and she knew from Brice's quick intake of breath, that he could see their outline through the tight garment. He moved further up the bed and Megan shifted her attention once again back to his hand. Now it was on her hip and suddenly Megan wanted to feel his hands everywhere.

Reaching down, she grabbed his wrist, pulling it gently towards her breast, equally fascinated by its movement as she was by her own boldness. Megan's lust was beyond her control, primal. Everything was one agonizing sensation after another, the sensitivity of her breasts, the heaviness in her groin. She could feel a pulsating hum move through her. It was just as Brice's hand cupped her breast, just as she arched into it, that it happened. A loud, retching noise. As though something were being strangled. Then, a wet hacking sound followed. Megan and Brice looked down at exactly the moment that Lucy vomited. On Brice's shoes. Both shoes. Horrified, Megan began to swing off the bed, but Brice held up his hand.

"No. Don't get up." She could hear the passion along with quiet resignation in his tone.

"You need ice on that ankle, and I need—well I guess I need new shoes."

Lucy stared up at Brice adoringly. There was a trail of drool still hanging from one jowl, her hind quarters swinging happily. She looked frustratingly adorable.

"Does she do that often?" Brice asked, as he gingerly slid out of his vomit covered shoes.

"Actually yes," Megan replied, sheepishly. "But only when she eats or drinks too fast. I'm afraid it's a regular occurrence around here."

"I will take note of that," Brice replied, laughing as he stood. "I'm going to grab some ice for your ankle." Looking down at his shoes he shook his head. "I have been looking for an excuse to get a new pair, so, Lucy," he continued, bending down on his haunches, "you actually did me a favor." To which Lucy promptly propelled herself onto his lap, slobbering all over him. Observing them together touched something deep inside of Megan. He really was a good guy. No, he's a great guy, she thought. After all, he clearly had the Lucy stamp of approval. What more could a girl ask for?

# CHAPTER 6

*I*t had been three days since the vomit incident. Before leaving that evening, Brice had made it clear to Megan that he had every intention of finishing what they had started, however, he insisted on taking her on a proper date. He was leaving the next morning for a convention out of state but would be returning that following Saturday. Which was tomorrow.

Tomorrow, Megan mused. She lay on her bed staring at the ceiling. Last night, sleep had been elusive. All she could think about was Brice and of course, where they had left off. To be honest, the fantasies regarding the latter are what had kept her up to begin with.

This would be their first real date, however, Megan felt she had known Brice forever. He was in her thoughts constantly, an ache that remained untouched. This was a dangerous man, she thought, one that made her think of what might be. What could be. Made her think of possibilities. Please don't let it be a disaster, she thought, glancing down at Lucy, the master of all disasters. One normal date. Just let me have one normal date.

Megan stared at her reflection as she sat on the edge of the bed. Her wet hair hung over one shoulder leaving a damp patch on her robe. She could see Lucy behind her, her rear end pointing towards the ceiling, her head buried under a pillow. She wasn't looking for anything, she simply liked this position. Megan's outfit of choice lay behind her, possibly the sexiest outfit she had ever chosen. The black and white sleeveless jumper clung to every curve, beginning with a plunging neckline that tied around the neck. She worried about the weight of her breasts; however, the salesgirl had assured her that the material was strong enough to keep everything safely in place.

Tonight, she wanted to be different. Wanted to step out of her comfort zone and explore this new sensuality that Brice seemed to bring out in her. Megan had never experienced anything like what she felt when she was with him. Everything in her world somehow felt brighter when he was near. Staring at her reflection, Megan hoped that Brice found her to be as beautiful as he made her feel, although truth be told, she had always believed that true beauty resided inside, emanating its special light outwards. Standing, she entered her bathroom, pausing a moment to begin the process of drying her long curly hair. It astounded her that anyone would think it was beautiful when she would much prefer her sister's gloriously straight hair. With a silent appeal to the universe that the evening went smoothly, she leaned back, looking over her shoulder at Lucy who had flipped from her rear end in the air to all four paws in the air. Smiling, Megan prepared for her special evening.

---

Brice paced back and forth from his couch to the bedroom and back again. After the third rotation he finally stopped, forcing himself to sit down. Turning on the television, he tried to relax himself. There was not a single time that he could remember ever feeling like this before a date. Yes, he had felt excitement as well as anticipation, but never this nervous energy. His bedroom looked like a tornado had ripped through it. Virtually every pair of pants, every shirt and practically every pair of shoes he owned were strewn around the room. Nothing he had tried on had seemed exactly right. In the end, Brice had opted for a classic pair of black pants, a plain black leather belt and crisp white dress shirt. A pair of black brogues and a splash of his favorite cologne completed the look. Brice knew that he was a good-looking man. Truthfully, he had never had a woman say no to a date and beautiful women approached him on a regular basis. Yet, it had never inflated his ego. Tonight, as he waited to pick Megan up, he wondered why this date was so different. She had a certain aura, as though there were a soft glow that seemed to hover around her. Of course, the bonus, the unexpected bonus, was Lucy.

"I'm even crazy about her dog," he said out loud, then laughed. Standing, he checked his watch and exactly one minute had passed from the last time he had checked it. Walking back to his room, he stood in the doorway examining the chaos, which at the moment, strongly resembled a crime scene. Once again glancing at his watch, he became convinced it was not moving. Deciding to use his nervous energy wisely, he set about putting his clothes away. Finishing up, he looked around one final time, satisfied that it no longer appeared as though a murder had taken place. Glancing at his watch yet again, Brice felt his stomach clench. This time the hands had moved. It was finally time to go.

Her sculpted figure was gloriously curvy. Brice attempted to drink her all in at once, but it was impossible, he realized. She was breathtaking. More than breathtaking. Stunning and ethereal. When Megan had opened the door no one could have prepared Brice for the gut punch that practically knocked him backwards. His senses competed to drink her in, from the lush, cascading curls that crashed to her waist, to the peaches and cream glow of her complexion. Even her sparkling eyes revealed her *joie de vivre*. As his gaze swept possessively over the rest of her, he felt his body tighten. Her breasts were magnificent, although now, they were spilling precariously from her outfit. When he was finally able to tear his gaze from them, the rest of her did him in completely. He couldn't help himself from caressing every line, starting at her delectable ribcage, to her flat stomach, ending as he observed the way the fabric of her jumper molded to her delicious thighs. Pulling his gaze back to her face, Megan was smiling mischievously.

"I will assume by that reaction that you like the outfit. Oh and," pointing to her feet, "I even have on flat dress shoes." Then, as he watched her appreciatively while she collected her purse and sweater, he suddenly heard a snapping sound, like a giant elastic. At the same moment the straps tied behind her neck fell forward spilling her breasts out. Brice stood frozen as he observed Megan's horrified expression as she attempted unsuccessfully to pull the material back up. Finally, he gathered his wits enough to push past her, then pulled a small blanket from the chair. Brice quickly wrapped it around her shoulders. Reaching over, he closed the door then gently guided her to the couch. He felt his powerful attraction rise to a dangerous level yet felt equally sympathetic to her acute embarrassment. It was then that Megan looked into his eyes and Brice was truly lost.

---

Reading his expression, Megan backed to the edge of the couch, her own breathing now rapid as she observed the stark need etched across his features. Nothing else seemed to exist except for this man, this moment.

"Do you have any idea what I want to do to you right now? How badly I want you?" She could see the force it was taking him to keep his hands by his sides, though she desperately needed to feel them on her.

"I think so," she whispered, ready when his lips devoured hers. Snaking her arms around his neck, she pushed herself against him. She couldn't get close enough. His arms circled her waist, then, cupping her buttocks, he lifted her, never losing contact with her mouth. Their tongues lashed at each other as though they had danced this way forever. As Brice pulled away from the kiss, Megan whimpered. The room grew cold without his touch and Megan was aware that she was tumbling towards a precipice, one she wasn't sure she was ready to cross over. It would require her to become vulnerable in a way that she never had, to open herself up emotionally, aware that a physical relationship with Brice would only irrevocably cement her connection to him. Yet, her body was clamoring for release, the pull of her passion taking the lead, pushing logic and reason aside. For the first time in her life, Megan was losing control and she didn't care. This was Brice and she wanted him, damn the consequences.

"Please, don't stop." It was all Brice needed to hear. He was vaguely aware of Lucy, who was observing them from her bed, moving her head from side to side as she listened to their sweet murmurings. Brice wanted to laugh at how comical she looked; however, he could barely manage the walk to Megan's bedroom. His legs were extraordinarily strong, but this woman did something to him. He felt like he did in high school. Out of control, not wanting to take his time. Brice wanted to bury himself in her now. Laying her gently on the bed, he turned, softly closing the bedroom door. He loved Lucy, but he wasn't taking any chances. Not tonight. Not with this incredible woman.

As Brice closed the door, he observed Megan through hooded lids. His heart was beating through his chest and for a moment he panicked. "She's so beautiful," he thought, as, standing at the foot of the bed, his impassioned gaze upon her, he slowly began unbuttoning his shirt, pulling it first out of his pants. When she sat up, he drew in his breath sharply, his eyes now free to rest on her magnificent breasts. A sea of flames moved quickly through Brice; unlike anything he had ever before experienced. Suddenly, he froze. What am I doing? he thought, as he stepped back from the bed.

With shaking hands, he started to put his belt back on. His face had a look of grim determination, as he came to a decision.

"I don't understand," Megan began, pulling the sheet up to cover herself.

Sitting on the side of the bed, Brice took both of her hands in his. His eyes, the color of a stormy sea, revealed that he was still fighting his desire for her. Taking a deep breath he spoke, his voice thick with unfulfilled desire.

"I want something more for our first time, Megan. Believe me," he continued, his voice uneven, "I want you. You have no idea how badly. But not rushed, not hurried. I want it planned and I want it perfect for you. You deserve the fairytale and even though I can't believe that I'm saying this," he continued, raking his hand through his hair in frustration, "I want us both to be ready. Heart and mind."

Brice watched as Megan processed what he was telling her, and he was desperately afraid that she would think he didn't want her when the real truth was, he wanted her badly enough to want to wait for it to be exactly as he hoped it would be. As they both hoped it would be.

"Please say something," he begged, squeezing her hands.

Megan leaned forward, kissing him gently. It was a different kiss, one that held the promise of tomorrow. Leaning back, she broke into a megawatt smile that hit him with a jolt. Brice couldn't remember ever seeing anything as beautiful as her smile.

"I'm hungry," she said. "Could you possibly feed me?"

Laughing, Brice rose quickly before he changed his mind. "If I stay in here for two more minutes with that beautiful body, I cannot guarantee that I will remain a gentleman," he said, swiftly closing the door so Megan could redress.

---

As she threw the damaged outfit into a corner, Megan couldn't help but be just a tiny bit happy that the straps had broken. I might even send the salesgirl a thank you note she thought, once again replaying the way his hands and mouth had felt. Steamy, she thought, shivering, definitely steamy.

Joining Brice once again, they finally managed to make it out of Megan's apartment. Once outside, she followed Brice to his vehicle. Brice had decided on dinner at a seafood restaurant in Portland that Megan had heard was great but hadn't had the chance to experience.

It was wonderful how easily the conversation flowed between them. Megan had changed into a periwinkle blue strapless summer dress, one that stayed securely where it belonged, grabbing a light sweater at the last minute, just in case. It was June, but the evenings could still carry cooler temperatures from the surrounding mountains. Arriving at the restaurant, they were seated immediately, Megan waiting as Brice pulled out her chair. Once they were settled, neither could stop talking. Later, Megan would wonder where the evening had gone, so immersed in their conversation that neither had paid much attention to the time.

As they walked out into the cool evening, Megan took a deep breath, looking up at the night sky as she did so. Glancing over at Brice she realized his gaze was focused on her, not the stars above. She felt the intensity of his eyes, her body responding immediately. Instantly her breasts tightened, and Megan closed her eyes seconds before his lips found hers. We haven't even made it to the car, she thought, as she molded herself more firmly against him, as though to absorb his body into hers. Megan broke away first, slightly surprised at her loss of control. Breathing heavily, Brice took her elbow, guiding her to the vehicle. Once inside, he quickly started the car. Pulling her sweater around her shoulders, she was touched that Brice must have noticed, as he quickly adjusted the heater.

Neither spoke as they headed back home, however the silence held no awkwardness. It was as though they both knew that this was a beginning. To what was yet to be determined, but Megan was excited to find out. When they finally arrived home, Brice stopped outside her door, making no attempt to enter. They kissed again and again; the passion ignited between them. This time it was Brice who broke the kiss. Leaning his forehead to hers he whispered huskily, "I need to see you again. Soon."

Smiling, Megan replied, her voice shaking with intense desire. "Me too. Very soon," and turning quickly, entered her apartment. Brice spun away and Megan watched him for a moment before quietly closing the door. Lucy looked up from her bed, her eyes sleepy, then rolled and stretched, her legs in the air. Megan slipped off her shoes, then, approaching her, knelt on the floor. Rubbing Lucy's belly, Megan listened to her pup's snorts of contentment as she tried to gain control over her own still palpable desire. There was little doubt that she was as attracted to Brice as he was to her. She also knew that she already missed him. One date, several amazing kisses and already she missed him. Instinctively, Megan knew that what she felt for Brice she had never felt for another man. It both excited and frightened her, yet she also knew that when he called again, and she knew he would, she would say yes to another date, and another and another. Absolutely, yes.

Brice did call again. And again, and again. Before she knew it, Megan knew that this man held all her heart. They still had not consummated the relationship, however, and she was determined that the next step would happen soon.

Brice's sister Amy was going to be back in town this weekend and they were planning on having dinner together. The evening of their dinner, Megan wore a pale blue sleeveless sundress peppered with tiny black flowers. A pair of flat black sling sandals and a light black sweater completed the look. She decided to wear her long hair down, its soft blonde waves tumbling down the length of her back. Standing in front of the bathroom mirror, she debated whether to wear makeup. Generally, she chose to be without, mostly because she was too lazy to bother, but tonight she decided on just a pinch of cheek highlighter, mascara and a pale pink lip gloss. With a final glance, she sighed loudly, wishing again for the millionth time that those freckles would go away, but, in all her twenty-eight years, they never had.

Megan had recommended a small Italian restaurant downtown, just two doors down from her store. She knew the owner and was able to get a reservation despite the short notice. Megan loved the quiet intimate atmosphere and felt they could all use some down time. They decided to meet at the elevator at seven and a few minutes before, she checked to be sure Lucy had everything she would need. Megan always left the television on for her. Animal Planet was her favorite. She put a few ice cubes into her water bowl, then freshened her food, adding a few extra treats. Bending, Megan gave her a quick kiss. "I will be back in a few hours," she said, rubbing Lucy's back. Then, looking into those soulful dark eyes, Megan bent one last time, hugging her tightly. Rising, Megan made one last cursory sweep around the room, assuring none of her shoes were left where Lucy could get them, then, blowing her a kiss, stepped into the hall quickly, locking the door. Glancing towards the elevator, she saw that neither Brice nor Amy was there yet. Opening her purse, she checked to be sure she had her phone. It was connected to a doggie cam so she could always see what Lucy was destroying when she wasn't home. Noting the phone was there, she turned towards the elevator.

Just as she started down the hall, Brice's door opened and the two stepped out. Amy waved enthusiastically, a bright smile on her face. Megan loved her outfit, a snappy red dress that hugged her curves in all the right places. Her shoes were adorable, strappy black sandals with just a small heel. Amy had opted for a messy updo, and her dark eyeshadow combined with bright red lipstick only further accentuated her exotic look.

While Megan admired her new friend's beauty, she felt no jealousy. She had long ago accepted herself, all her perfect imperfections. Well, she thought, except for the freckles. They really did drive her crazy. Moving forward, Megan, who had been busy admiring Amy's outfit, suddenly shifted her attention to Brice.

He looked ridiculously beautiful she thought, admiring how fit he appeared in a camel-colored button-down shirt tucked into dark brown slacks. She could just see the dark hairs above the line of his shirt. Her breath caught as she tried to take him all in. Megan didn't realize that she had stopped walking and was now openly gaping at Brice. She literally couldn't take her eyes off him. but she wasn't the only one staring. She observed him as his eyes swept over her deliberately, his expression intense, laser focused. The realization that she had this effect on Brice only intensified Megan's attraction. Something in the way his body seemed to physically tighten, as though he were prepared to spring towards her, his intention obvious and unapologetically sexy. Megan was barely aware of Amy's existence, so fixed on Brice that she was surprised when she finally became cognizant of her outrageous behavior. Finally, she turned and observed Amy, leaning casually against the wall, her expression amused.

Slightly mortified by her behavior, Megan continued forward until they all stood at the elevator; Amy, the only one with the wherewithal to hit the down button. Megan noticed Brice dabbing his forehead and wondered why he was sweating. If anything, the condo building maintenance kept it close to freezing.

Trying to brush off her strong attraction to Brice, which Megan absolutely knew would be impossible, she decided instead to appear as unaffected by him as she reasonably could. Once on the elevator, Brice smiled at her warmly and that, combined with the fact that whatever cologne he was wearing made her want to lick him, convinced her that appearing unaffected would also be impossible. She decided then that all she could do was try not to be an unsophisticated, besotted wretch and get through the evening, hopefully, relatively unscathed.

# CHAPTER 7

$\mathcal{T}$he restaurant was busy but not noisy and Megan mentally congratulated herself on her choice. Soon they were seated and had ordered drinks. Thankfully, Amy's constant excited chatter broke up the sexual tension between her and Brice. She felt his piercing gaze several times, leaving her with a raw sense of her own femininity. He made her feel exquisite, as though he found her unique, precious.

Dinner arrived and Megan was grateful for the interruption to her chaotic emotions. She was also starving and ate with her usual enthusiasm. No shy flower when it came to her appetite, Megan dug in, finishing everything on her plate plus part of Amy's.

Afterwards, they ordered coffee and by now Megan felt completely relaxed. The conversation flowed and Megan genuinely admired both Brice and Amy, coming from the children of immigrants who had arrived in America with very little money and unable to speak English, who had persevered, instilling in their children a strong work ethic. It was wonderful to hear their stories and to gain insight into the kind of man Brice was. He was most assuredly rare. The conversation turned to travel when Amy mentioned that she would be leaving for Italy in a few months on a much-anticipated vacation.

"Oh, I am so jealous!" Megan exclaimed, her eyes lighting up with excitement. "I have never been anywhere outside of the United States." Glancing over at Brice, she asked, "Have you travelled anywhere interesting?"

Nodding affirmatively, Brice answered. "Actually, I have been to Europe and Asia several times, but I guess you could say I left my heart in Thailand."

"Oh," Megan replied, "how so?"

Before he could respond, Amy interrupted, tossing her brother a loving smile. "Brice has done a great deal of volunteer work in several countries helping the indigent with their dental care," she said, pride evident in her voice. "His heart is as big as he is."

"I only volunteered a few times," he replied humbly. "It wasn't a big deal really, but there was one particular village," he continued, his expression grim. "I have never seen so much suffering. I knew that I needed to help somehow so I arranged to travel back with some colleagues. It was the most rewarding experience I have ever had," he finished.

Megan once again identified that now familiar heat rush through her, the attraction raging, unyielding. The knowledge that he had a heart for people only ignited the fire into an inferno.

"So, I decided to sign on for two years," she heard him say. Lost in her thoughts, she had missed what Brice was saying.

"I'm sorry, what did you say about two years?" she asked.

Amy answered. "Well, my magnanimous brother decided after his contract expires here at the end of this year, he's going back to Thailand. There's a wonderful organization that he signed on with," she boasted, casting an adoring look at her brother. "He has volunteered two years of his life to help the people of the Napar Village."

If it were at all possible for one to feel one's heart drop to the floor and then climb into one's shoe and then nestle under one's arch, then that is exactly what Megan felt upon hearing that Brice would be leaving. Two years, she thought, suddenly despondent.

Trying to regain her composure, Megan attempted a smile. Unfortunately, she looked more like the Cheshire Cat. Observing the startled expressions coming from both Brice and Amy, she dialed it back to something a bit less psychotic. In a shrill voice that was overly enthusiastic, she twittered, "How wonderful for you! I mean how wonderful for them as well, since you are a fantastic dentist, which I know of course, because you're my dentist," then, with a short bark, she grabbed her water glass. Taking a deep gulp, she promptly began to choke.

Slamming back his chair so violently that it toppled over into the table behind him, surprising a gentleman who, unfortunately, had chosen that exact moment to raise his wine glass to his lips, spilling it onto his very white dress shirt, Brice rushed over to Megan. He lifted her from her chair by her armpits so forcefully that one of her shoes flew off onto a neighboring table, arriving like a slam dunk into a young woman's soup. Brice then proceeded to thump so hard onto her back that the water in question came back out, projecting across the table, hitting Amy square in the chest. Megan watched as though everything were happening in slow motion. She could see the shocked as well as concerned expressions of the other diners, the waitress as she furiously tried to wipe the customer's wine-stained shirt, the poor woman trying to wipe the soup out of her hair. Amy, poor Amy, with a large damp spot staining her beautiful outfit.

Closing her eyes, she took some deep breaths. Brice spun her around, holding her against him. Megan quietly placed her head against his chest. It was as though it had found home, that she had found home, in his arms.

While she stood there, she tried to remember a time in her life when she had felt this humiliated. Slowly, she steadied her breathing to match the rhythmic beats of his heart as she prepared to leave the safety of his arms. Megan looked up into Brice's insanely celestial eyes, sympathy practically oozing out of them, and because she simply didn't know what else to do to salvage what small amount of self-respect she had left, she began to cry. As if the last five horrific minutes were not enough, now she was crying.

Amy rushed over and gently guided Megan through the restaurant, out onto the sidewalk. Brice was inside settling the bill, which, no doubt, included two additional dinners, a glass of wine, and one expensive white dress shirt. The two women stood, silent except for the occasional small shuddering breath as Megan's eyes, directed towards the mountain summit, fought for control of her traitorous emotions. Finally, she faced Amy.

"I have no idea what happened there. I am just so sorry to have embarrassed you both. I seem to be doing that with a great deal of regularity," she finished apologetically.

"Oh, you have no need to feel badly," Amy responded gently. "We are quite used to all of the loud noisy displays of life. In fact," she continued, smiling kindly as she observed her brother emerge from the restaurant, "we really quite prefer it!"

Not sure whether she truly believed her, Megan felt her heart speed up as she met Brice's eyes. Coming to a stop directly in front of her he clasped both of her hands, his expression one of concern.

"Are you feeling better?" he asked, gently rubbing both of her palms with his thumbs.

"Aside from a case of extreme humiliation I am," she replied, a tremulous smile crossing her features. Megan was trying to ignore the frisson of excitement climbing her spine as he continued to massage her hands.

"Good," he replied, gazing at her intently. "You scared me to death."

"Me as well," Amy chimed in, gently steering Megan down the

sidewalk towards home. The sudden loss of Brice's touch left Megan feeling somewhat forlorn. It was such an odd sensation that she decided she would analyze it later. For now, she simply wanted to go home and digest the news that Brice was going away for two years.

Two years was such a long time, and he would be thousands of miles away. Suddenly, she felt tears once again threatening, however, mercifully, they had arrived back at the apartment complex.

Entering the elevator together, Megan was grateful for Amy's conversation as it once again covered the awkwardness that had suddenly arisen between her and Brice. Relieved when they finally stepped off onto their floor, Megan quickly thanked them both, then, waving abruptly, she quickly let herself into her apartment. Megan knew she was being borderline rude, but she simply wouldn't be able to handle another minute before she further embarrassed herself. She let out a quick sigh of relief as she leaned against the door, closing her eyes.

Feeling a wet nose she bent, giving Lucy her customary greeting consisting of a hug, followed by a quick kiss on the top of her furry head. Satisfied with Megan's greeting, Lucy meandered back to her bed, small spurts of gas following her.

Shaking her head, a smile playing around her lips, Megan slipped off her shoes, tossing them into her closet as she entered her bedroom. All she could think of was a long hot shower. She didn't want to dissect the evening or replay the horror. Slipping off her clothes, she stood still as the hot water travelled over her, the tension that had been present slowly beginning to ease. Afterwards, Megan wrapped her hair in a towel, then retrieved her favorite robe from the foot of the bed. It was just as she was preparing a hot cup of tea to further relax her, that Megan heard the doorbell ring.

Startled, she looked at the clock on the stove. It was 10:30. As she approached the door she observed Lucy, ears perked at full attention. In stealth mode, she placed her eye against the peep hole. It was Brice. What was he doing here? she wondered wildly. Then, without thinking, she swung the door open. Megan could see Brice's eyes widen as they skimmed over her body. It suddenly occurred to Megan that she was standing there in nothing but her favorite robe, worn and faded from use, with a towel wrapped around her still very wet hair. Reaching up, she self-consciously tried adjusting it.

Brice just stood, staring at her, his eyes again combing over her body, finally coming to rest on her lips. Megan could feel the shift in her, a primal sensation that pulled her into his arms. His mouth crushed hers, his tongue forcing its way inside, dancing furiously with hers. He tasted like wine and kindness.

Somehow, they were inside as Brice slammed the door shut with his foot. He had spun her so that her back was pressed against the door. His hands were everywhere. She allowed them to roam freely, completely at his mercy. She didn't want to think, only feel.

As though they had a life of their own, Megan's hands, too, began their own exploration. Her fingertips ran along the back of his neck then slowly down his broad shoulders. She allowed herself a brief pause as the power in his solid forearms communicated themselves to her, the muscles undulating beneath the layers of his clothing. Then, slowly, she allowed them to splay across his abdomen. She felt him tense, heard his sharp intake of breath, his nostrils flaring. At that moment Megan had never felt more power. They brushed along his ribcage, and it was then that he pushed himself more firmly against her, his hard thighs now flush with her body.

Brice's mouth left her lips, his breath hot and uneven against her neck. He parted her robe revealing her breasts, taut with desire. It was only when she felt his tongue on her nipple that Megan suddenly panicked. Pushing him away, she quickly closed her robe, tightening it around her waist. She fought to control her rapid breathing. Looking across the room, she spotted Lucy, perched in the corner of the couch, head cocked to one side. Brice, too, was trying for control and as she stepped around him, their eyes met.

"I'm not sorry," he rasped, his voice thick and uneven. "The truth is, I can't seem to get enough of you." Megan smiled, her heartbeat finally slowing down from a gallop to a walk.

"Me too," she admitted. Walking the few steps to the couch she sat, watching as he placed himself across from her.

"Why did you stop?" he asked softly.

Breathing deeply, she answered.

"You're leaving, Brice. For two years. It's something you should have mentioned before I—before now," she finished. "I have a life here, a business I have worked hard to grow, a family. I can't go with you, and you can't stay. I won't start something that will only break my heart. I'm too much of a coward."

Bowing his head, Brice spoke quietly. "You're right. I should have told you. I wanted to, many times, but I was afraid of—"

"Of what, Brice? Afraid of what?"

"Of this. This conversation. You possibly ending it."

"'Ending it? Have we even started it?"

His expression bleak, he said, "I'm not leaving for several months, Megan," a note of desperation in his voice. "I haven't even received my departure date yet. Why can't we continue to see one another?" he entreated. "I believe we have started something. This thing between us is real. It's not just about sleeping with you either," he continued earnestly. "I feel a deeper connection and I know you do as well."

Megan felt her resolve slipping as she listened to his argument, her eyes straying to his lips. Still, it was because of the depth of their connection, that she knew the ending would be an inevitable heartbreak. She would be a fool to continue the relationship knowing there could only be one outcome. As if sensing her pain, Lucy quietly climbed onto Megan's lap, laying her head gently on her stomach. Inhaling deeply, Megan released the air on a sigh.

"No, Brice. I'm so very sorry. Please understand my position. It stops here. It stops tonight."

With a slight shake of his head, Brice rose, a look of sad resignation on his face. Gently moving Lucy, Megan stood as well. With only a nod in her direction, Brice walked to the door then, his hand on the knob, he turned. Speaking quietly over his shoulder he said, his voice husky with desire, "I respect your feelings, Megan. I guess I even understand them, but I for one will always wonder what could have been."

Without responding, Megan watched as he let himself out quietly. Falling back onto the couch, Megan placed her hands over her face as she allowed the tears to run unchecked. She had never felt this way about any other man and certainly never so quickly. He was dangerous to her heart and Megan knew she simply couldn't see him again. No matter what. Later that night she lay wide awake, staring at the ceiling as she listened to Lucy's gentle snores. She was positive she had done the right thing. Then why, she wondered just before she finally found sleep, does it feel so wrong?

# CHAPTER 8

"*A*re you out of your mind?" Lindsey shrieked, practically falling over the flower shop counter. "I mean seriously! You allowed him to walk out just like that," she continued, snapping her fingers loudly.

"How many times do I have to say this?" Megan responded defensively. "He is leaving. The country. For two years!" she bellowed, holding up two fingers as though that might somehow drive home to her sister why she would unequivocally not see Brice again.

"So what? He said he isn't leaving for several months. Anything could happen in the interim," she continued, following Megan to the back of the shop as she checked on her flower supplies.

"Really? Like what exactly? Hmmm. Oh, wait I know," she continued sarcastically. "I could fall even more madly in love and lose myself entirely and discover day after day just how absolutely perfect he is for me? Like that?" she continued, jamming roses into a glass vase.

"Well, no, not exactly," Lindsey stated. "It's just you haven't even given him a chance. What if he changed his mind and stayed?" Rolling her eyes, Megan turned and walked back to the front of the shop, Lindsey on her heels. Standing behind the counter, Megan reached down, grabbing a bag of Lucy's treats. Alert to the familiar sound, she sprang from her bed in the back, sprinting to Megan's feet. Staring up at her, tongue falling from the side of her mouth, she waited patiently for her snack.

"That's just it, Lindsey," Megan exclaimed, waving the treat in the air, Lucy's eyes following it like a cat on a laser light. "I wouldn't want to be the person responsible for him not pursuing his dream. He is donating two years of his life to help indigent people get good oral care. He is giving up his entire life to help them. I do not want to be the woman who stops that from happening. I couldn't live with myself."

Hesitating, Lindsey finally responded. "Ugh, fine," she fumed, snatching the forgotten treat from Megan's fingers. "When you put it that way, I guess I get it. But I don't like it," she continued, as she leaned down to give a now impatient Lucy her much anticipated snack. Seizing it, Lucy turned, trotting back to her bed, a noxious haze following in her wake.

"Whoa!" Lindsey gasped, waving her hands frantically in front of her face. "What did you feed her last night?" Pulling up the bottom of her shirt, she placed a corner to her watering eyes.

Sighing heavily, Megan once again bent down, this time retrieving a can of room freshener, spraying somewhere in the direction of the rear of the store.

"Well since I cannot get you to change your mind about that incredible hunk of dentist that has fallen at your feet, then my mission is over, although," Lindsey emphasized, "I do not accept defeat." Retrieving her purse, she headed to the door.

Smiling, Megan replied. "I would expect nothing less from my most determined sister." As she grasped the door handle Lindsey turned, her expression somber. "I know you want to do the right thing Megan. You always do. But just once I would love to see you follow your heart. Jump in. Take a chance. I have seen the look on your face when you talk about him. You are much braver than you know," she continued as she opened the door, stepping onto the sidewalk. "Just think about it Megan. Please."

Blowing her a kiss, Megan nodded.

"I'll definitely give it some thought," she promised.

Coming out from behind the counter, Megan walked to the window, watching until Lindsey was out of sight, then long after. She had replayed last night in her head repeatedly, but the ending was always the same. Brice was leaving. She was staying.

Tonight, Megan and Lindsey were planning to have dinner with her parents. They all tried to get together at least once a month to catch up. Megan looked forward to the distraction.

She still felt that she was doing the right thing, although she had unwittingly found herself attempting to figure out a way that being apart for two years could actually work. Since Brice would be unable to travel back here, she would need to travel there if they were to see each other at all. She would need to find someone to run the store as well as care for Lucy for at least two weeks. Travel time alone would account for four days. Plus, she could only do that once a year. No matter how she spun it, they would need to commit to waiting to resume a normal relationship for two years. Megan just didn't know if she could, or more to the point, could Brice?

The remainder of the day was fruitful as her business was especially busy in the summer months, yet not busy enough that Brice didn't cross her mind at least once every five minutes. She couldn't help wondering if Brice thought of her as well.

Later that evening, Megan sat back, her hand rubbing her full stomach.

"I cannot believe how much I ate," she groaned. "I will be big as a house if you keep feeding me like this, Mom."

"Oh hush. You could use a good home-cooked meal now and

again. I know that you and your sister," staring pointedly at Lindsey, "tend to eat pizza most days. That or fast food."

"I love pizza," Lindsey replied, enthusiastically. "I really could eat it forever!"

"Exactly what I thought," her mother replied, beginning to clear the table. The two girls joined her. Their father was attending a golf tournament with friends, so tonight it had been just the girls. After the kitchen was cleaned, all three ladies walked out onto the back porch. Evenings in Maine, even in summer months, could be cool, and tonight was no exception. They all had wrapped sweaters around their shoulders, then settled into their favorite chairs.

Megan, leaning her head back, closed her eyes, relishing the fresh breeze wafting down from the mountains, enjoying its gentle caress. The sun had not completely set so she could still feel its warmth. She listened to her sister and mother chatting. Her thoughts, however, were far from here this evening. Instead, all she could see was Brice's bold features. Her mind wandered to his hands and then to the rest of him. Soon, her reflections became so intense, that she began squirming uncomfortably in her chair.

"Are you ok Megan?" she heard her mother ask. Startled from her reverie, she cleared her throat, sitting up straighter as she did so.

"I'm fine. This chair just feels a little hard."

Lindsey looked at her curiously, "Have you told Mom about Brice yet?"

Eyes widening in panic, Megan shot Lindsey a murderous look, shaking her head no. Her mother, seated between the two girls, volleyed back and forth between them.

"Wait, what? Who is Brice? You haven't said a word," her mother accused, shooting Megan the dreaded 'mother look'.

"Oh, good grief, Mom, there isn't really anything to tell. He moved in down the hall from me, that's all. He's just a neighbor."

"He's her dentist too," Lindsey teased, smiling widely in Megan's direction.

While her mother's attention was on Lindsey, Megan mouthed 'I'm going to kill you', which Lindsey clearly did not find threatening in the least.

"He's your dentist?" her mother shrieked, placing her hand dramatically over her heart. "What happened to Dr. Kilbran? He didn't die, did he?" she whispered, her expression worried.

"Oh no, of course not!" Megan replied, momentarily taken aback. "He retired so he and his wife are travelling a great deal. You know, what retired people do," she finished, shrugging.

"Anyway!" Lindsey boomed, causing them both to jump. "We were talking about Brice, remember?"

Sighing loudly, Megan turned towards them both.

"Ok, Ok. Here it is. I actually really like this man."

Lindsey's eyes widened, her I-told-you-so expression crossing her features. Meanwhile, her mother began clapping her hands together in glee. They really are too much sometimes, Megan thought. Rolling her eyes, she continued.

"The thing is, Mom, he's leaving soon for a two year stay in Thailand. As a volunteer," she finished, unable to keep the note of regret from her voice.

"Oh, I see," her mother responded, sympathetically. "Well, what are you going to do?"

Megan had been weighing that repeatedly since her last conversation with Brice. She couldn't stop thinking about him. How he made her feel, his laughter, his kindness, all of it. It had been twenty-four hours and she couldn't do it. She couldn't stay away from Brice. It's utterly ridiculous, she thought.

"Well, I guess I'm just going to jump in," she announced, completely unaware until that moment that she had made her decision. If they only had a few short months together, then she was determined to love him every second she could. "I don't know how it will all unfold," she whispered, "but I have to try."

"Yessss!" Lindsey cheered, jumping from her chair. Rushing over, she folded herself over Megan, hugging her tightly. "I'm so proud of you," she said happily. "I'm going in to get a drink. Anyone want anything?"

Both she and her mother shook their heads, quietly watching as Lindsey made her way in. Once they were alone, her mother reached over. Taking her hands, she searched Megan's face.

"Are you sure you want to do this, knowing he's leaving? You have nothing to prove to any of us. If you don't want to pursue this, as much as your father and I want to see you happy and settled and bounce a grandbaby or two on our laps, and we really, REALLY want to bounce a grandbaby," she continued emphatically, "your wellbeing comes first. I know it's occurred to you that you could very well be left with only a broken heart."

Listening, Megan knew everything her mother was saying was the truth. She also knew that whatever this was that drew her so strongly to this man, it was greater than her fear of heartbreak.

"I know, Mom, but I'm absolutely sure that I'm willing to take the risk."

Squeezing her hands one last time, her mother stood, Megan joining her. The two walked back in, the air now too cold for comfort. They spent the rest of the evening talking about hair, the best skin moisturizers on the market and what foods they could eat in excess without gaining any weight. They never came up with an answer for that one.

Once home, Megan tried to think of the best way to tell Brice that she had changed her mind without making her appear to be a complete nitwit, although, truthfully, she felt the ship may have already sailed on that one. She decided to call, and upon receiving his voice mail, left a message asking him out on a date. After she left the message, she realized that she hadn't explained why she was asking him out on a date, when the last thing she had told him was that they could never, in fact, go out on another date. Pacing, she was trying to come up with a way of calling a second time without appearing psychotic or stalkerish when her phone rang. It was Brice. Frozen, she just stared at the phone, then, before she could chicken out, quickly answered.

"Yes," she heard him say, before she could speak.

Laughing, Megan felt relief wash through her.

"Good," she replied. "When—"

"I have to work tomorrow," he interrupted. "The office took Saturday hours. However, I will be off by five. I will pick you up at seven." He hesitated a moment then continued, "'I was thinking perhaps we might plan a getaway. I know you're busy with the store, but I think you would really enjoy it."

"I just might be up for that," she replied, excited at the prospect.

"Great. I'll see you tomorrow then. Oh, and wear your sexiest outfit with no breakable parts."

Laughing out loud, Megan agreed. After they hung up, she walked over to the couch where Lucy observed her, bright eyes twinkling with doggie happiness.

"Well, it looks like your favorite person will be here tomorrow," she stated, in between dropping kisses on Lucy's forehead. Come to think of it, she realized, grabbing a soft drink from the fridge, then settling down next to Lucy, he may very well be my favorite person too.


Megan left early the next morning for the store knowing it was Saturday and usually one of her busiest days. At least she hoped it was. She was full of pent-up energy which most assuredly was of a sexual nature so keeping busy would help. She was counting on it. Megan couldn't wait to feel his lips everywhere and was hoping his hands would join in. Lucy was in rare form this morning and it had taken an exorbitantly long time to arrive at work. Her desire to become best friends with a lizard had resulted in Megan gently extricating said lizard off the side of Lucy's jowl. It had then attached itself to her finger and the whole process began again. Several passersby had found it amusing and decided to video the event. Megan, on the other hand, had not been amused. Breathless from half jogging half walking while carrying Lucy, Megan finally fell through the shop door. As she had anticipated, it was extremely busy and before she knew it, it was four o'clock. Finalizing her last few orders Megan heard her cell phone ring. She smiled when she saw that it was Lindsey.

"What do you want, brat?" she answered laughingly

"Just checking in. Anything special planned with anyone special that I should know about?"

"Hmmmm. Well, it just so happens that a certain dentist has asked to take me away."

"What? When? Where? Oh, I'm so excited!"

Grinning, Megan answered. "I'm not sure. We're going out tonight and he said he would tell me then."

"So, I take it he was happy to hear from you?"

"Thankfully, yes," Megan answered, unable to contain the relief in her voice. "He's picking me up tonight but mentioned he thought we should plan a getaway."

"Oh, you had better tell me as soon as you know!"

"I will," Megan answered happily.

"Don't forget! You always forget!"

"I promise, I will not forget. Now hang up. I have to work."

"Call meeeee!" was the last thing she heard as she hung up.

# CHAPTER 9

*B*rice was taking her camping. Camping.

Two days later Megan sat cross legged on the floor of her bedroom as she looked at the various articles of clothing strewn about. A small suitcase, lying a few feet away, had some warm socks and underwear packed in it, along with a few sweaters and some jeans folded off to the side. It was only going to be two nights, but Megan had no idea what she should bring.

Although she had been raised in the northeast, her parents were not outdoorsy people unless swimming in resort pools and golfing counted. Megan and Lindsey had both been hiking and had enjoyed that very much, however, that was quite different than sleeping outside. In the woods. Where all the animals were. Oh, and spiders and snakes and crawly things. At the thought, Megan shivered. It hadn't occurred to her until just then what she had agreed to.

The sound of scratching interrupted her thoughts. Turning, she observed Lucy trying to dig her way to China via the suitcase. The socks and underwear were no longer packed. "Lucy!" Megan admonished, exasperated. Hearing her name she stopped, then squatted, throwing Megan a resentful toss of her head. Her frustration evident, Megan was preparing to stand when she heard the key in her front door. She knew it had to be Lindsey who she had given a spare key to in the event of an emergency. Megan heard the keys hit the table and looked up as her sister walked into the room. Lucy, always happy to see Lindsey but also trying to teach Megan a lesson, opted to swing her behind in excitement as she folded herself once again into the suitcase. Clearly, she was not yet ready to concede her position as it pertained to the luggage.

Lindsey stopped just inside the door, taking in the scene before her.

"You never called me," she stated, her voice accusatory.

Looking over, her expression guilty, Megan apologized.

"I know. I'm sorry. It's just been crazy at the store and well... It just slipped my mind."

"Humph," Lindsey replied, her way of saying she forgave her. "If you're getting rid of clothes I want the first pick," she said, her voice excited. While they were different heights they wore the same size, so very often they would exchange tops and jackets.

"I'm not getting rid of anything," she answered, as her sister sat on the edge of the bed facing her. Reaching down, she rubbed Lucy's head in greeting.

"So where is Brice taking you? Bahamas? Aruba? I'm dying to know," In the same breath, she continued, "Do you ever wear that top?" pointing to one of Megan's favorite summer blouses.

"Yes, I wear it often, and no, you cannot have it and no, you cannot borrow it because I think I'm wearing it."

"Ugh. Ok. So where are you guys going? I'm so jealous, by the way," she continued, her voice wistful. "I bet he's whisking you away to some romantic tropical location where they serve delicious fruity drinks and there are gorgeous thick robes in the closet."

Shaking her head, Megan chuckled.

"You would be wrong. He is taking me camping."

"Camping?" Lindsey replied incredulously.

"Yes, camping," Megan replied, nodding.

"But have you ever been camping?"

"Well, no, bu—"

"Do you like camping?"

"Well, I don't kn—"

"Are you aware that there are things that could literally eat you out there?" Then, a look of horror crossing her features, she continued, "You aren't taking Lucy, are you? She could get eaten too. She is the perfect snack size," she ended with a wail.

Glancing over at Lucy, Megan observed her worried expression. "Nothing is going to eat you, silly. Don't listen to her."

"Also, poisonous snakes and spiders that I'm pretty sure can fly."

Holding up her hand, Megan interrupted the litany of beasts capable of killing them.

"I'm sure we will be absolutely fine. Brice has camped his entire life and is very knowledgeable. I'm positive he will keep us safe. Plus, I really want to experience it," Megan continued. "I'm actually looking forward to it. Well, mostly," she admitted sheepishly. "I mean I'm a little bit nervous. Lucy is coming, of course, but will be by my side the entire time."

"Oh, I have no doubt about that at all," Lindsey replied. "I just really never thought of you as the camping type. But I'm glad you're going and still doing the whole jump in thing," she finished, enthusiastically.

"When are you two leaving?"

"In a few days. I just needed to wrap up a few loose strings at the store and Brice had to get coverage. Tonight, Brice invited me to meet one of his colleagues that he will be volunteering with in Thailand. I was wondering if you would like to join us? It would be a great opportunity for you to get to know him better."

"I would love to!" she replied happily.

Scooting over to the suitcase, Megan gently deposited Lucy

onto the bed, once again placing socks, underwear and a small pile of sweaters back in. Lucy, with a final reproachful glance, raised her head, exiting majestically from the room.

Both women looked at each other and laughed.

"She is so dramatic," Lindsey chortled, waving her arms expansively.

"Yes," Megan agreed, nodding affirmatively. "Every single day."

The invitation to go camping had been a surprise to Megan. When Brice had asked at dinner she had hesitated. Brice had taken that to mean she didn't want to go and had instantly started to apologize. "I'm sorry," he said. "It's too soon. Of course. I should have known."

Horrified that he had gotten the wrong impression, Megan had quickly assured him that she had merely been surprised but that she would love to go. They had made the arrangements and Megan felt like she was walking on air. Thankfully, she had considered that she would like to take vacations and of course, emergencies do happen, mostly since she had acquired Lucy, so Megan felt exceedingly grateful that she had the forethought to hire a wonderful college student who was willing to work occa-sional weekends and some weekdays should Megan need her. In fact, she had already worked the Saturday Megan had met Gabby in the park and had done wonderfully.

Their dinner had been sexually charged and Megan didn't taste anything she ate. Rushing back, they had just arrived at Megan's door when Brice received an urgent call. A colleague's daughter had been in an accident.

After he hung up Brice pulled her towards him, his forehead resting against hers. "I don't want to leave," he whispered, his frustration evident. "It appears something is always pulling me from you when all I want to do is be with you."

"I know, Brice. I feel the same way."

Pulling back, he stared deeply into her eyes. "I love everything about you, Megan. I love your intelligence, your humor, your kindness. I love that you love family as much as I do. The whole incredible package," he finished, leaning in to kiss her cheek gently.

She could see that Brice was torn, but Megan knew that the right thing was to send him on his way. "You'd better go," she said, "I know they need you right now. Plus, I get to see you tomorrow night. But first," she whispered, pulling him towards her, "let me leave you with this." She brought his head down, kissing him passionately.

The following evening, as planned, Megan and Lindsey prepared to meet Brice at the same Italian restaurant that Megan swore she would never return to. Lindsey was very excited, although Megan was suspicious that it had more to do with eating pizza than in getting to know Brice. Megan, on the other hand, had ambivalent feelings about the evening. She wanted to be supportive, as she could see how much it meant to Brice for her to meet his Thailand colleague, but ultimately his departure could also be the reason that she and Brice might have to end their relationship. Whoever this colleague was, Brice obviously thought very highly of them, so Megan really wanted to make a good impression. Brice was going straight from work to the restaurant so after Megan gave a quick tidy to the room and placed a kiss on Lucy's forehead, the two women headed out.

The fleeting colors of dusk dipped below the horizon high-lighting the charcoal black rocks of the distant summits. Breathing deeply, Megan relished the cool air after the high temperatures of the day. Both women had opted for loose summer pants and sleeveless tops, but both had brought along sweaters. As they began walking, Megan wrapped hers around her shoulders while Lindsey carried hers loosely over one arm.

Upon their arrival they were seated, Megan excusing herself to use the restroom. Brice had texted he would be there in just a minute so she gave Lindsey the job to keep a lookout, informing her that he would be the tall dark man wearing a pale gray sweater, something he had brought to her attention, the result of a conversation in which Megan had mentioned how much she loved the color on him. Taking a few extra minutes to touch up the sparse amount of makeup she was wearing while attempting to tame the mass of chaotic curls that were reacting very badly to the humidity, Megan finally gave up.

As she approached the table, Megan suddenly faltered. Brice was standing next to an extraordinarily beautiful brunette. The woman was speaking animatedly to Lindsey and as she came up beside Brice, he turned to her, his face lighting up with pleasure. Glancing over, her sister gave her a sympathetic look. It was then that she gave the stranger her full attention. She appeared slightly older than Megan. She was also quite tall, almost exactly shoulder to shoulder with Brice. Her legs went straight to heaven and the rest of her was equally sublime as revealed in the form fitting skirt and molded blouse that she wore. Megan couldn't detect a single flaw. Not that I'm trying to, she told herself, mentally shrugging. From the perfectly shaped eyebrows, over-looking expressive coffee-colored eyes, to the aquiline nose that rose just slightly above the most perfectly plump lips Megan had ever seen, she was a vision. She had not escaped the attention of any of the males in the restaurant, most of whom were eyeing her surreptitiously. The women were trying to ignore her altogether.

"Megan Cunningham, this is Sarah Mayers." Brice stated. "Sarah, this is Megan."

Placing her hand out, Sarah's grip was firm. Her smile was open and friendly, revealing of course, perfect teeth. Megan suddenly felt ashamed. This wasn't like her at all. Although, truthfully, Brice could have prepared her. He had never mentioned that his colleague was a woman. A very stunning, insanely perfect woman. After ordering drinks, the four sat back, Brice reaching over and squeezing Megan's hand, leaning in for a quick kiss. Megan felt an immediate electric current run through her at the contact as well as a certain level of relief. The pit in her stomach was still there but manageable. This woman would be in the same small village as Brice. For two years. Together. Lindsey, horrifyingly enough, unabashedly stared at Sarah with a kind of hero worship that Megan had never seen before, asking her question after question about what she used on her hair and skin and for goodness' sake did she just ask her where she got her outfit? Megan tried desperately to control her irritation, refusing to recognize it as jealousy.

As the evening wore on it became clear to Megan how important this woman was to Brice. They gravitated to each other consistently and while the topic was always work related, they had such an easy rapport, leaving little doubt to Brice's fondness for her. It was unmistakable.

The evening finally ended with Megan breathing a sigh of relief. She had tried to find some fault with Sarah, but she had been gracious, kind and engaging. Once outside, they stood for a few moments to the side of the restaurant entrance, saying their goodbyes. Brice was going to drive Sarah back to the office where her roommate would meet her, since Sarah's car was in the shop for repairs.

Leaning in close, Brice whispered in her ear. "Can I stop by later?" His breath was hot against her skin, and she shivered with need. The sensations coursing through her body were raw, primal.

"Yes," Megan gulped, trying to drag in the air. With a quick nod, he moved away, and Megan watched as he placed his hand on Sarah's elbow, guiding her to his car. It was shocking how much that bothered Megan. Seeing Brice's hands on another woman caused an inward cringe. Turning abruptly, she began walking back. Lindsey, catching up with her, let out a low whistle.

"Clearly you had no idea Brice's colleague was a woman," Lindsey stated. "I mean it was obvious." Startled, Megan stopped mid stride.

"Great. If you noticed, then so did Brice, and of course the beautiful angel from on high did as well, I'm sure. Ugh!"

Turning, Megan began walking again, Lindsey falling in beside her.

"I mean I noticed, but I'm your sister and I know you. I'm positive neither Brice nor Sarah picked up on it." When Megan remained silent, Lindsey continued. "You know, I was watching Brice and that man never took his eyes off you. I have never seen anyone so completely besotted."

"Well except when he was talking to Sarah which was all night," Megan replied, her voice dripping with sarcasm.

"Wait," Lindsey breathed, incredulously, "You're not jealous, are you? You have never shown an ounce of jealousy with any other man. Even when you had reason to."

Entering the building, Megan didn't answer, but once in the elevator, she simply felt deflated. Slumping against the wall, she closed her eyes briefly.

"I know," she whispered. "This isn't me. I don't know who I am when I'm around him," she continued, opening her eyes. Lindsey's look of concern touched her.

"I will be fine," she continued. "Really. I guess when I jumped in, I never really thought of the actual effort there would be to keep swimming."

As the elevator doors opened, they stepped out. Reaching the door, Megan let them in, then made her way immediately to the couch, slipping her shoes off as she fell back onto the cushion.

Lucy, loudly yawning while she whined, rolled unceremoniously off her bed, then standing, slowly ambled over to lay at Megan's feet. Sitting across from her, Lindsey smiled.

"It must be love," she affirmed as she too slipped off her shoes. Bringing her legs up she folded them underneath.

"Maybe," Megan replied. "I feel all jittery when I'm with him, but in a good way. I can't explain it really," she continued, her tone frustrated. "Only that, with him, I see forever. I have never felt that way before, not even with Paul."

Lindsey's eyes widened. Paul had been Megan's first love. They had been together during the latter part of high school through her first two years of college. Unfortunately, Paul had met someone else, and Megan had found out not from Paul, but from his new girlfriend. It had taken months for Megan to get over the breakup and there were times that Lindsey worried she never would. However, Megan was an extraordinarily strong woman and a determined one, so eventually she was back out there, although there had been no serious boyfriends since.

"He's coming over soon and I would like to bring up the subject of Sarah but the last thing I want is to appear needy or jealous, which I have been feeling all evening."

Shaking her head emphatically, Lindsey spoke firmly. "Don't you dare. He is coming here to you. Certainly, if he wanted Sarah, he would be with her."

Megan knew that this was not who she was. If Brice wanted her then it would happen in the right timing, but she refused to be in competition with anyone else for his attention. That, she knew, was a slippery slope. Her beauty, she believed, was intrinsic as well as unique. It was something her parents had repeated to their children many times. Relaxing, she glanced over at Lindsey sheepishly.

"I have been acting like a complete lunatic, haven't I?"

Nodding, Lindsey stood, sliding into her shoes.

"Yes, but you're such an adorable lunatic. Just promise me you will not bring up the subject of Sarah unless he does."

Sticking out her pinky finger, Lindsey wrapped hers around it, both girls squeezing gently.

"Pinky swear," they both said in unison. Laughing, Lindsey walked to the door, Lucy following. Bending over, she gave her a customary goodbye kiss. Satisfied, Lucy trotted back to her bed, whistling gas as she did so. Both women quickly waved their hands in front of their faces, Lindsey doing so until she stepped onto the elevator.

After she left, Megan went into her bedroom, slipping into a pair of sweats and a plain white t-shirt. Making her way back to the kitchen, she grabbed a bottled water then settled onto the couch, Lucy on her lap. "Try not to cause a ruckus tonight," she said lovingly, leaning down to kiss her head. "Because if anyone can," she sighed, "it's you."

# CHAPTER 10

*M*egan tried to relax yet knowing that Brice would be here soon caused nervous anticipation. They were leaving in the morning for their camping trip and Megan wasn't entirely sure which she was more excited about. His arrival this evening or their trip tomorrow.

Alone with Brice in the woods, she thought, a shiver of excitement raising goosebumps along her arms. She knew that Brice wanted their first time to be special, but Megan wasn't sure how much longer she could wait. As it was, every time he was near, she wanted to launch herself like a torpedo onto him. There was a specific vision she kept running through her mind that involved strawberry preserves and caramel sauce, which Megan wasn't entirely sure might not be just shy of psychotic. Either way, that she knew of, there wasn't a '1-800 what's a normal sexual fantasy' hotline available. Glancing over to the pantry door where she kept those items, she shook her head. "Too soon," she thought. Definitely too soon.

Rubbing Lucy's belly, Megan allowed herself to let her imagination run wild. In her mind's eye she pictured them, wrapped together in a cozy tent, a soft light coming from somewhere.

Here, she faltered, as she had no idea what one used for lighting in the woods. Pushing past that, she closed her eyes, leaning her head back against the cushion. Now Brice was slowly removing her top, one button at a time, except she was pretty sure that wouldn't be the top she would be wearing. Brice had mentioned she should wear thermal tops at night and since this was happening at night, in the soft glow coming from an unknown light source, he wouldn't be unbuttoning the top. He would be lifting it off her. Settling once more into her imagination, she watched as Brice pulled her top gently over her head, revealing her sexiest bra. Again, she stopped, realizing how idiotic it would be to be wearing a black lace bra tied with several ribbons and bows out in the middle of the wilderness. But then again, why not, she reasoned. Smiling, she allowed herself to go back, leaving the black ribboned sexy bra on.

Without taking it off, she imagined him cupping her breast, squeezing gently as she arched herself towards him. She could feel the material gently rub her skin. Snaking her arms around his neck, his hands traveled down her ba—

The knock at the door startled Megan. Jumping up quickly, Lucy rolled haphazardly off her lap, her nose landing in the corner of the couch. Quickly rolling her back out, Megan ran her fingers through her hair, no doubt making it worse. Taking a deep breath, she opened the door. He stood there, the cool night air still clinging to his jacket. Smiling lazily, he stepped in, gently closing the door behind him.

"Come here," he growled, pulling her into his arms. Standing on tiptoe, she wrapped her arms around his neck, allowing all of her to press into him. She could feel his need, hard and hot against her. His mouth was everywhere, devouring her, as she met his passion hungrily. Stumbling backwards, they made their way to the couch.

Looking over her shoulder, Megan saw that Lucy had not moved. She was in corpse mode. Megan mentally screamed with frustration. Stepping from Brice's arms, she lifted Lucy's motionless body, gently laying her on her bed. With a resentful huff, Lucy stood, then spinning three times, flopped back down in a full doggy snit.

With a sigh of relief, Megan turned her attention back to Brice. He was sitting on the sofa, legs spread slightly apart. Crooking his finger, he patted the couch next to him. Feeling suddenly brazen, Megan shook her head no. With a look of anticipation, Brice watched, eyes narrowing as she slowly approached, then, pushing his knees together, she straddled him. He leaned his head back, his eyes heavy with desire. Both were breathing heavily, their mutual passion for each other palpable.

Moving her lips over his, Megan thrust her tongue into his mouth, an action that demanded he reciprocate. His hands slipped under her shirt, cupping her full, taut breast. Slowly she began to rock herself over him, his desire hard against her. His breathing was rough, choppy and Megan knew they were almost at the point of no return.

As if he knew her thoughts, Brice suddenly placed his hands on her hips, halting her movement. She leaned her forehead into his, astounded by the depth of her need. Neither spoke, only waited for their hearts to resume normal rhythm. Sliding off him, Megan sat, curling her legs beneath her as she rested her head on his shoulder. He raised his arm, sliding it behind her possessively as she burrowed deeper into his side. She could feel the tension pulsing through him. Megan knew that he was using every ounce of control he had to stop himself from finishing what they had started.

"I told myself I would just stop in for a glass of wine and leave, but there you were," he said, his voice a low rumble, "Looking so beautiful."

Embarrassed, Megan glanced down at herself. She was so in the habit of slipping into her relaxed garb that she had done so almost without conscious thought.

"I'm wearing sweats and my father's old t-shirt. Hardly my sexiest look," she finished. "I'm afraid that while I do love a cute dress and sexy heels, I much prefer comfortable clothing at home."

She felt his hands gently caress her head, his fingers idly combing through her hair.

"You are breathtaking no matter what you have on, which I think we both know, is quite evident. Is still evident actually," he finished, shifting as he tried to get more comfortable.

"Brice, about that. I know that you said you wanted it to be special, and I love that you want that, but the truth is, I think it would be special no matter when it happens. We only have a few months left together, and, well…" her voice trailed off.

Shifting slightly away, Brice placed his finger under her chin, gently forcing her face up. His eyes were still filled with desire as well as something else, something that Megan couldn't quite identify.

"I wish I could drag you into your room and have my way with you," he said, his voice a low growl, "but right now, at this exact moment, my best friend from college is in my living room. He flew here to surprise me. Since you and I are going away tomorrow, I'm afraid tonight is all he and I will have to catch up."

"Wait. What?" she exclaimed, pulling away. "When were you going to tell me that?"

"I meant to tell you right away but then I saw you, all sexy and gorgeous and I couldn't help myself," he insisted.

Suddenly, Megan burst out laughing. "You and I have the worst luck ever," she chortled. Glancing at him lovingly, she nodded. "Of course, you should go," she sighed, kissing his cheek. "But be here all the earlier tomorrow," she demanded, punching his arm playfully.

Kissing the top of her head, Brice stood to go. Gathering her in his arms, he held her tightly. Megan could hear his heartbeat, and nothing had ever felt more like home. He was only going down the hall and she would see him in the morning, but she already missed him. After a deep kiss, Brice left her, with a feeling of intense disappointment at war with her unfulfilled passion.

Closing her door, Megan leaned back. Inhaling deeply she attempted to stem the raging desire that coursed through her. She had never wanted anyone the way she wanted Brice. It was now a mantra that played repeatedly in her mind, a consistent need that echoed throughout her body. Megan wondered not for the first time when their mutual desire would finally be brought to fruition. Restless, she made her way to the couch, curling up with her favorite blanket. Turning on the television she tried to distract herself, only to turn it back off a short time later in frustration. Lucy, sensing her shift in mood jumped up. Shifting, Megan welcomed her furry warmth as she lay along her side. They stayed this way late into the evening until Megan gently rose, and carrying Lucy, made her way to bed, her dreams, when she finally slept, of Brice.

As Brice made his way back to his apartment he tried to work through his emotions. Thus far everything in him wanted Megan, in every way. Still, the knowledge of his imminent departure continued to nag at him. The truth was he was nervous to take the next step, although he wanted desperately to become intimate with Megan. The fact that he knew she felt the same made his reticence even more frustrating. If he were completely honest, he would admit that there was a level of embarrassment as well. Megan must be questioning why they had still not proceeded to the next level of their relationship.

Pausing in the hallway, he took a moment to gather himself. While he was happy his friend had taken the trouble to stop in unexpectedly for a visit, Brice just wasn't feeling a boisterous round of guy talk. What he really needed was to sift through the plethora of sensations he was experiencing to try to make sense of them all. Megan deserved complete transparency and now, he felt he was still holding back. Brice was determined to be open and honest with Megan and desperately hoped this camping trip would give him that opportunity. The truth was he had been practicing what he would say to her, afraid that it would come out the wrong way, that he might hurt her. When he was with her everything got jumbled up inside. This incredibly strong physical attraction was difficult, almost impossible to control. Yet, Brice equally admired her intelligence, her keen wit and her extraordinary sense of humor. Megan made him better when he was with her, made him want to BE better. He also knew that this was something unique in his life. There had never been another woman who had ever had this effect on his senses. Still, as nervous as he was about what he knew he must share, he was equally excited at the prospect of their trip. Because all Brice really knew for sure was that he needed Megan. That, he thought, was everything.

Morning sun flooded the apartment causing Megan to blink as she shuffled into the kitchen for her coffee. She had tossed most of the night, unable to stop thinking about Brice. When he arrived at her door promptly at seven, she was more than ready to go. Lucy, on the other hand, was not feeling terribly energetic and Brice ended up carrying her to the elevator, then to the truck. He did so happily though, and it warmed Megan's heart to witness his abject kindness towards Lucy. He would be an excellent father, she thought, feeling a sudden frisson of excitement at the idea of having Brice's children. She could almost feel her ovaries screaming to get started right now.

As they drove toward the campground, Megan couldn't get

over the extraordinary beauty surrounding her. The air was crisp, carrying with it a soft breeze, wrapped in the scent of sunshine. While at times unpredictable, the forecast was pointing to a calm weekend. Both Brice and Megan were looking forward to relaxing in the beauty of the mountains.

Peeking over at Brice, Megan couldn't help allowing her eyes to drink him in. His faded jeans, while not tight fitting, clearly outlined his muscular legs. His dark pullover hugged his arms, the collar resting just below his ears. Sensing her stare, he glanced over at her, a knowing grin on his face. Turning his attention back towards the road, he chuckled.

Aware that she had been caught, Megan felt the flush climb her neck, then spread itself over her face. She was trying desperately to keep her thoughts on the beauty outside of the vehicle. The fall colors really were spectacular, and Megan drank in the vivid yellows, greens and deep purples of the foliage. Despite having lived here her entire life she never got enough of the extraordinary vista the changing seasons elicited.

---

Brice was glad he was driving because he was pretty sure, had he not been, he would have spread Megan out over the back seat and plunged into her by now. His body was screaming for release. For the first time since signing on to the Thailand Clinic, Brice felt unsure he had made the right decision. His honest self-analysis last night weighed heavily on his conscience. He had every intention of fulfilling his obligation, although the idea of leaving Megan in a few months hurt him in a way he had not been prepared for. Yet, he couldn't stop seeing her. It was selfish of him, he knew that. He knew he would have to leave her and while he didn't know the true depth of her feelings for him, he knew she was as attracted to him as he was to her. Their chemistry was off the charts and Brice knew that when they finally came together it would be explosive.

This time his heart was leading, and he was scared to death. He even had grown attached to Lucy and when he allowed himself to consider a future with Megan, Lucy was in it. Flatulence and all. Brice didn't know how, but he was determined to find a solution to their situation. He knew that he couldn't possibly ask her to wait. Long-distance relationships invariably caused more pain and Brice wasn't willing to do that to either of them. He thought that there just had to be a way, but time was running out. Fast.

# CHAPTER 11

he campground was deserted when Brice and Megan arrived. After locating their spot, they assembled their tent, meaning Brice assembled it. Returning from a short walk with Lucy, Megan observed Brice as he climbed out of the tent. Watching him unfold, her breath caught. Brice smiled brilliantly in her direction, then, sauntering over to where she stood, wrapped his arms around her.

For long sweet minutes they teased each other with their tongues, allowing their hands to caress at will. They were surrounded by trees and completely alone. The nearest campers were over a mile away. Megan permitted herself to have her fill of him. Running her fingers through his hair, she pulled his head down more firmly as she sought to get closer. It was as though she were starving, and Brice was the feast. She felt his hands cup her buttocks. Instinctively she raised herself up, then, as he lifted, she wrapped her legs tightly around him. Slowly she began to rock, sliding against him, feeling his hardness through her sweatpants. She was more than ready for him. His breathing was harsh as he whispered into her ear. With a thrill, she realized he was speaking in Spanish. She had almost forgotten he was Cuban. That, his body, the male hardness against her, were her undoing. The climax hit her hard as she buried her head into his neck, convulsing against him.

Megan was both relieved and embarrassed at her complete lack of control, yet the tension had been building in her since the first moment she had crashed into him. Slowly, she slid down his body, his chest vibrating with laughter. Looking up, his eyes were brimming with desire, but too, she thought she recognized something else. Something deep and tender.

---

"I'm so embarrassed," she began, but he quickly interrupted.

"There is nothing to be embarrassed about. It was damn hot and probably the sexiest thing I have ever experienced. It was beautiful and so are you," he ended, kissing her forehead gently.

Stepping back from his arms, Megan smiled sheepishly.

"Well, if you ever want me to return the favor," she trailed off, grinning wolfishly.

Chuckling, Brice smiled down at Megan. She had no idea how badly he wanted to finish this, but he knew, especially with his own confusion, that to do so before he talked to her about his own reservations would be unfair, to both of them.

"Oh, I will definitely be asking for that favor to be returned. But right now, maybe we could go on a hike? I need to get rid of some excess energy," he elaborated, adjusting his pants.

Laughing, Megan replied. "Deal! I'll go grab my boots out of the truck and meet you back here in five."

Heading back to their tent to grab some water bottles, Brice marveled at his self-control. He would be lying if he didn't say he felt pretty good that he had given Megan pleasure and was glad that she didn't know that he himself had been mere seconds from his own climax. Thankfully, she had stopped moving when she did, otherwise Brice didn't think he could handle the embarrassment. He prided himself on his self-control and had always been able to give a woman pleasure before himself, as well as having the ability to hold back his own pleasure until he was ready. Today, however, with Megan it was different. He had felt all his restraint slipping, as though it were his first time. While there had not been many women, Brice was an experienced lover, although with Megan, he felt like a schoolboy. It was humbling and frightening at the same time. He knew that he was in even deeper than he realized, as he gathered the water and snacks from the cooler near his sleeping bag. While he knew he had feelings for Megan, he was only just beginning to realize how deep they were. Brice had never believed in love at first sight, but he knew, in that moment, that the petite blonde with the gassy dog waiting for him outside his tent was the woman for him.

He loved her.

It astounded him and rocked him to his core. But he had no doubt. However, instead of the joy it should have given him, Brice felt fear. How was he ever going to be able to leave her? Should he end this now, he wondered, as he tied his boots. He instantly rejected the thought. She was like oxygen to him. No, he was too selfish to be able to let her go. Not now. "Let me just have the next few months," he pleaded to the tent rooftop, raising closed eyes. Just not yet. Just not now.

Megan had Lucy in a pooch pouch. Shaking his head, Brice's shoulders shook with laughter as he approached.

"I was wondering what we were going to do with her," he said, pointing to Lucy, who was panting joyously. Megan smiled widely.

"Well, she won't walk, and I couldn't leave her here, so," she finished, pointing down the front of her chest. It was a cool contraption, Brice noted. Two straps went around Megan's neck and two more around her waist. The pouch had a small shelf at the base, so it appeared sturdy enough to hold Lucy's weight.

---

Soon they were on a well-marked trail. Thirty minutes into their hike, they approached a deep stream that spilled gloriously from three steep waterfall ledges. Brice helped Megan take Lucy out, who snorted happily and immediately bounded forward. Brice held her as Megan firmly attached her leash to the harness, double checking it was secure before letting her move out further. Lucy wandered, sniffing her surroundings, occasionally cocking her head at the sounds of the forest. Soon enough she had exhausted her reserve of energy, the result, no doubt, of being carried everywhere, and all three settled happily under a large oak. They were quiet for some time, the beauty of their surroundings enveloping them. Even Lucy seemed delighted as she lifted her nose to catch the wondrous new scents carried by the mountain breeze. The waterfall was mesmerizing, and Megan was surprised that she could still hear the birds as they traversed the tree branches above them. The air was cool but not cold. Megan couldn't remember a time that she had felt this content. Glancing over at Brice, she was startled by his intense gaze. Immediately, the air became electric between them.

"Megan," Brice began haltingly, "I know this probably isn't the best time to bring this up but I feel like we need to discuss my move. I'm leaving soon, as you know, but it must be apparent that I have developed feelings for you."

Megan's heart began to race. She, too, felt strongly for Brice but she was petrified that he had taken her up here to break it off. She knew how honorable he was, and it would be just like him to try to save her from the pain of his inevitable departure.

Shakily she replied. "Yes, I know, Brice, and I'm sure it hasn't escaped your attention that I return those feelings. I mean, I'm trying to catapult myself onto you every time we're together," she finished, shrugging her shoulders.

Chuckling, Brice smiled widely.

"It's definitely not escaped my notice and to say I'm flattered would be an understatement. In fact," he continued, sliding over to be closer, "that's kind of what I wanted to talk about. I want to take this to the next step, Megan. I want to wake up next to you. I want to be inside of you. I can't think straight anytime I'm around you and frankly, even when I'm not, you're in my head."

"I know. I feel the same way," she whispered.

"But I'm leaving, Megan. For two years." Taking a deep breath, he continued, his expression troubled. "The fact is, once we arrive at the village, we aren't able to leave again. Its remote location makes it virtually impossible to visit back and forth. There must be so many doctors available at all times and unfortunately, it isn't a place where you can find coverage." Swallowing hard, she watched as he struggled with what he had to say next, her own stomach doing sickening flips.

"I have also learned," he continued, his voice low, "that there are no visitors allowed on the compound itself. I read it in the contract I signed but that was before I met you. Otherwise, please believe me, I would never have agreed to those terms." Shaking his head, he looked into her eyes, regret brimming from their depths. "I don't want to hurt you. I know you can't come, and I must go. So, I guess what I'm asking is, are you willing to go all in, knowing the difficulties that lie ahead?"

Taking in a shaky breath, Megan hesitated before answering. She thought she had been more than ready to become intimate with Brice, but suddenly, she wasn't sure anymore.

Because now, she realized, now she was in love.

She loved Brice and the realization shot through her like lightning, its power jolting. The knowledge also brought a moment of deep fear. Would becoming intimate make the separation even more difficult, she wondered. Already she knew that she would miss his presence, the sound of his laughter, his keen wit and humor. How much more punishing, then, would it be to add to that the loss of his body, his touch, the feel of him beside her in bed? Megan could feel a sense of panic envelop her and she instantly recoiled from it. Once again, she felt her frustration at their situation rise.

Megan simply wasn't sure that adding a physical relationship, despite her love for him, would be the right thing to do. She realized she had no reference point for what was happening and instinctively Megan felt she should take some more time to decide what would be best for herself as well as for Brice. She didn't want to hurt him, but her heart felt fragile.

Finally, Megan cleared her throat and her heart softened at the look of expectancy as well as fear on Brice's face.

"I need more time," she breathed. "I thought I knew, thought I could do this, but I wasn't thinking about the ending. I guess I was trying to pretend it wasn't going to happen." Sighing heavily, she continued. "So, could we just have this weekend? I know that I want you Brice, that should be abundantly clear. But I do need to think about what moving forward in a physical relationship will mean for me, emotionally. I hope you can understand that. I don't want to hurt you, Brice. I will make a decision after we get back from this trip, I promise."

Brice smiled lovingly and Megan's breath caught. She wanted to tell him she loved him but that would be too cruel. He was leaving and she couldn't do that to him. Wouldn't do that to him.

After that, they both relaxed, trying desperately to enjoy their time together. That evening, after pan-frying fish and smores by the fire, they each went to their separate sleeping bags, both staying up all night, thinking about the other. Thinking about their inevitable goodbye.

---

Once home, Megan felt utterly lost. After helping her in with her supplies, Brice kissed her gently at the door. Holding her, he whispered, "I won't call you or come over. When you're ready, I will be waiting, and Megan," he continued, stepping back and gazing gently into her eyes, "there is no wrong answer. I want you to choose what will be best for you. It's important to me that you know that."

Gulping back tears, Megan could only nod as Brice left, gently closing the door behind him.

That day Megan had allowed the tears to come, unchecked. Lucy, sensing her pain, was well behaved, instinctively aware of Megan's mood. Her phone was turned off and she binge watched every romantic movie she could find that had a happy ending while simultaneously screaming at the stupidity of the happy ending. All while eating mounds of Rocky Road ice cream. She was buried under a mountain of blankets on the couch, hair tangled, stray pieces that defied gravity sticking out inches from her head, when she heard a key in the front door. Moaning, she pulled the blanket over her head. Hearing the keys hit the counter, she waited. Gently, she felt the blanket being pulled down, stopping at her nose. Lindsey's worried eyes warmed her heart. With a heavy sigh she sat up, swinging her legs to the floor. She was wearing her Jedi slippers and at Lindsey's amused expression, she shrugged.

"They're my favorite," she remarked, smiling sheepishly.

Without saying anything, Lindsey sat across from her sister and waited.

"I can't see Brice again," Megan announced, her voice determined.

When Lindsey didn't respond she continued

"I thought I could, but, I mean, two years," she moaned. Slapping her hand to her forehead she continued her tirade. "Who does that anyway? Not me," she answered, pointing somewhere south of her chest. "I'm no idiot. My heart will be broken and for what?" Not waiting for an answer, Megan continued.

"My life was perfect before that Cuban dentist with his gorgeous everything injected himself into my life with his ridiculous niceness! The very least he could have done was to be selfish, or a jerk, or I don't know what, but the thing is—" tears sliding down her cheeks, "the thing is, Linz," she whispered, "I love him. I actually have fallen in love with him."

Lindsey stood, making her way over to the couch. Sitting next to Megan, she enfolded her as she cried deeply and silently into her shoulder. They stayed that way until Megan gently pulled away, wiping her face with the sleeve of her sweatshirt.

Standing, Lindsey made her way to the kitchen. Reaching into the refrigerator, she grabbed two bottled waters. Handing Megan one, she opened hers as she sat across from her once again.

"That's a big deal, Megan," Lindsey said, her expression serious. "You have never said that about anyone. Not even Paul. Are you sure?" Without waiting for an answer, she continued. "You haven't really known each other that long," she finished, her expression searching.

"I know. Believe me," she replied, taking a large gulp of water and swallowing. "I have tried to talk myself out of this feeling. But it's like nothing I have ever felt before. I want to wake up every day for the rest of my life next to him. I want to watch our beautiful children, who will, no doubt, look exactly like their father, running to greet him as he comes home after a long day. I want to share every single sunrise and every single sunset with him. That's how I know," she finished, her voice subdued. "Because all of that lives in here," she whispered, placing her hand over her heart.

"Ok, so what's the problem, again?" Lindsey inquired, with a chuckle at Megan's incredulous expression.

"He. Is. Leaving," she enunciated each word slowly. "For two," here she held up two fingers, just so Lindsey understood how many two was, "years," she finished, her irritation showing.

"And? That means?"

"That means," Megan spat out, "that means that my heart will already be broken anyway, but if we are together, you know, *in that way*, it will be so much more disastrous! Just pure disaster and how will I survive it?"

"I wish I could tell you what to do Megan. It must be your choice and I know; I KNOW that you will make the exact right one for you. I know that because you are my big sister, you are my best friend, and you are extraordinarily strong. I love you sis and I'm here whenever you need me. I could stay tonight, maybe run home and grab a few things and be back before dinner? Cook you a healthy meal," she continued, glancing over at the pizza and ice cream boxes.

Megan knew Lindsey had exams coming up and loved her all the more for offering, despite her own busy schedule.

Megan shook her head.

"No, I truly will be fine," she replied, as she gazed around the room, straightening her shoulders.

"I have allowed myself enough sadness. My decision is made, and I will stick by it. I think it's best, and by the way," she continued, casting Lindsey a loving glance. "Have I told you lately what an awesome little sister you are?"

"No, but I'm always up for hearing how amazing I am!"

Both women laughed as they hugged and shortly afterwards Lindsey left, promising to come back on Friday night for pizza and a movie. Megan couldn't resist peeking her head out the door towards Brice's apartment and felt a stab of disappointment when she didn't see him. Megan decided that she would stop by his apartment tomorrow after work. She felt that she should give him her decision in person. Also, she couldn't imagine not seeing him again. It was selfish, she knew, but vital. To feel his arms around her, his kiss, all were imperative, even for just a moment, because Megan knew that she needed that moment to last a lifetime.

# CHAPTER 12

*T*he next day the sun was shining, the birds were singing, and she had a rush of customers throughout the morning. It was the kind of day that she normally loved but today she only felt a heaviness. The world was darker today, she thought morosely, staring unseeingly out the store window. The mist had rolled off the mountaintops, revealing the rugged peaks, yet even that had failed to lift her spirits. Even Lucy was quiet, her normal excitement at visiting with customers was significantly subdued. It was as if she knew what Megan would be doing tonight. Saying goodbye to Brice. Just the thought brought tears to Megan's eyes. Wiping them away impatiently, she squared her shoulders. Enough, she chided herself. You're doing the right thing. No need to keep crying into your cheerios for crying out loud.

She was headed for the back room to replace her ribbon supply when she heard the bell chime announcing a customer. Turning, she stumbled slightly, eyes widening. It was Brice's colleague. The stunning colleague. Sarah. She was dressed differently, Megan noted, wearing a pair of form-fitted faded jeans and a simple sleeveless top. Her flip flops revealed perfectly manicured toes and Megan could not help looking quickly down at her own. She had missed her last pedicure appointment, so basically she felt that comparatively, she had claws with color. Megan also noted that instead of her hair being down, gloriously cascading around her beautiful face as it had been at dinner, today she had her straight thick hair pulled back in a simple ponytail. "Equally as gorgeous," Megan thought, sighing inwardly. Instinctively, she tried to smooth down her riotous curls. Reminding her that they had no intention of cooperating, they bounced right back. Lucy had already approached Sarah who was bending, running her perfectly manicured hand down her back. Standing, she sent a blinding smile towards Megan. Megan couldn't help returning the infectious greeting.

"I'm not sure you remember me—" Sarah started, as she stepped further into the store, taking in the flowers arranged in the large refrigerators.

"Oh of course I do," Megan replied. "I'm so glad you stopped in."

"I was just out shopping, and it popped into my head that you had a flower shop here. Brice has mentioned it and you often," she finished.

Not sure what Brice had told her about their relationship, Megan decided to keep that to herself. It was over anyway, she thought sadly.

Noticing the downcast expression on Megan's face, Sarah was quick to apologize.

"I'm so sorry," she began. "I didn't mean to upset you."

Embarrassed and once again reminded that she did not have a poker face, Megan recovered quickly, sending Sarah a warm smile.

"Oh no, not at all," she responded. "I'm glad you stopped in. I love showing the place off," she bragged, waving her arm expansively. "It's really my Shangri-La."

"I can see why," Sarah replied. "I love these old historical buildings. I wanted to be an archaeologist. I decided that dentistry might pay more bills, but all things old are really my passion," she finished, smiling down at Lucy who was now sitting on her foot.

"Lucy!" Megan admonished, scooping her up as she apologized. "She has literally no concept of personal space," Megan announced, as she kissed her forehead.

"Oh, it's fine," Sarah stated. "My fiancé has a golden retriever named Max, and truthfully if I weren't leaving for two years, I would definitely want another. I love dogs," she finished, casting a loving glance towards Lucy.

Megan barely heard her. "She had a fiancé?" The news hit Megan like a slingshot to the forehead. Suddenly, she felt elated. Sarah was getting married. To someone else, Megan thought, marveling at how light she felt. Yet it was short lived as she quickly remembered that it didn't change anything. Brice was still going to be gone for two years. Two long years.

Megan, realizing suddenly that Sarah was still talking, tried desperately to catch up.

"So unfortunately," Sarah finished, "he won't be able to come to Thailand. I'm just really worried," she continued, "if I'm being completely truthful."

"'Because your fiancé can't visit you in Thailand you mean?"

"'Exactly," she replied. "He is a dentist at a different practice just a few miles away. We both signed on for the Thailand Clinic" she explained, "except he wasn't chosen, having signed on past the deadline. When we realized what happened I immediately told him I would withdraw my name, but he wouldn't have it. Ryan is like that, though," Sarah continued, her face softening. "He would never allow me to sacrifice my dream."

"But aren't you afraid to be separated for so long," Megan asked, unable to help herself. "I just know if it were me," she continued, her voice subdued, "I wouldn't know how to handle such a long separation."

"I'm not looking forward to it," Sarah replied, her tone forlorn. "But unless we could find another dentist willing to cover the breaks then we won't be able to cover the time off, which is a part of the conditions to being accepted to the program. It's voluntary, but believe it or not, much desired not only for its altruism but also for the tremendous experience we will gain. Our future patients will certainly benefit," she continued, "Sadly, there aren't many willing to forgo income for such an extended period, so coverage is virtually impossible," she sighed.

Megan felt terrible. She had allowed herself to feel jealousy which she simply didn't believe in to begin with, and this amazing woman was sacrificing not only her paycheck but also would have to separate from the man she loved. It occurred to her how terribly selfish she had been.

The two women spoke for a few minutes longer and after purchasing a small plant for her office, Sarah left. Impulsively, Megan hugged her as she stepped out the door.

"I think you're wonderful," Megan gushed. "Please feel free to come anytime."

Waving gaily as she walked down the sidewalk, Sarah promised to come back for another visit soon.

Closing the door, Megan leaned against the counter, expelling a deep breath. She still couldn't believe how wrong she had initially been when she had first met Sarah. She had simply made a quick judgment based on her own insecurities. Surely it was a lesson on getting to know someone based on who they are, not on how they look.

Megan was reflective the remainder of the day, her mood subdued. She was dreading the end of the day and was slower than usual on the walk home.

After she arrived, she made herself some soup, although she had no appetite. Her stomach was in knots but finally she knew it was time. Grabbing her key, she glanced over her shoulder as she headed to the door. Lucy was standing by her dog bed, her expression downcast, as if she knew that Megan was about to break her own heart.

The walk to Brice's door was too fast and she found herself standing in front of it, fist raised. She stood this way for several moments, then, sucking in a deep breath she knocked. The door opened so quickly that she was startled. Brice scanned her face, his own revealing his anxiety.

Without speaking, Megan stepped in and slowly walked to the couch, sitting at its edge. Brice sat across from her, leaning forward, his stare unwavering. He waited for her to speak. Megan drank him in. He was so handsome. So very beautiful. She knew that Brice was rare. A man of honor with deeply held convictions, a desire to help those less fortunate. He was also strong, his virility, even now, a palpable thing. She observed the thick cords in his neck, observed his bounding pulse and knew that his heart was beating as quickly as hers. As she opened her mouth to speak, the words that came out were as much a surprise to her as they were to Brice. In those precious moments of contemplation, Megan realized that life wasn't something she needed to outsmart, or to control. That you were given gifts rarely and oh how rare was this man? She knew that; indeed, the true tragedy would be to let him go one second before she had to. They had precious little time left, yet they could still share sunrises and sunsets, lazy mornings and steamy nights. Megan knew that if that was all they would ever have, it would be worth it.

"I realized," she began, her voice low and full of love, "that I would rather have a minute of extraordinary than a lifetime of mediocre."

They both stood and Megan walked into his open arms, her head resting against his broad chest. In this moment she was the most vulnerable she had ever been, her every cell in tune with Brice. She breathed him in for a few more seconds, then taking a step back, looked up into the stormy seas of his eyes. There, she could see his love, not hidden or held back, but instead, a precious gift that he offered.

He bent his head, his lips gentle at first, tasting her as though it were the first time. In a way, Megan believed that it was. It was a new kiss, the first that they shared knowing that they were stepping into an unknown future together. Brice gathered her up and walked into his bedroom. Megan was ready with no reservations about her decision. She watched through heavily lidded eyes as Brice began to undress. He never took his eyes from her and when he was finally naked Megan was overwhelmed by his masculine beauty. Every inch of him was hard lines and powerful pulsating ripples.

Slowly he began to unbutton her blouse and Megan couldn't help but think how far from reality her fantasies had been. "This is so much better," she thought, moaning when she felt his hand cup her breast. She didn't remember how the rest of her clothes came off, only that finally the moment had come, and it was hard and fast, their bodies slick with their mutual desire. His tongue advanced over her flesh slowly, hot, leaving a trail of goose-bumps as he slowly made his way to her core. His fingers sepa-rated her, and she thrust upwards, her head tossing on the pillow from side to side, all control gone. His tongue was hard when it announced its presence, his hands cupping her buttocks, kneading them while he made love to her open mound. Her climax lasted for minutes and was so strong that it was almost painful. Then he was above her, his fullness taking her breath as he thrust manically. He sought her mouth and she tasted herself there and it was too much as she joined him in another shat-tering climax. She watched Brice when he finally found his relief, observing the shudder run down his body. When he opened his eyes, he looked stunned, and sexier than any man had a right to look. Rolling off her, he gathered her close against him, their bodies returning slowly to normal. Megan never wanted this night to end, never wanted to leave the sanctity of this moment.

Brice was the first to speak.

"I love you," he said simply, but his voice was determined. "I was afraid to tell you, but you should know that. I love you."

Tears gathered in Megan's eyes. Raising herself up on one elbow, she looked into his eyes.

"I love you, too. I have for some time," she whispered, leaning in to kiss him gently on the lips. "No matter what," she breathed, "I will always love you." Though it had been mere minutes, the passion between them flared again and Brice pulled her so that she lay across him. Their kisses became fiercer as Megan undulated over Brice. When he entered, she gasped, the fullness spiraling her into yet another climax with Brice's own following just moments later. It was as though they couldn't get enough of each other, and the rest of the evening was spent making love, until finally, in the early morning hours, they fell asleep in each other's arms, each unsure of what their future held, but willing to face it, good or bad, together.

The next week was full of abject joy for Megan. There had been no awkwardness the morning following their first night together. It was as though it were always meant to be, that they were meant to be. Soon, aside from work, they were never apart. Megan knew she was headed for a devastating fall, but her love for this man was everything. There was no turning back.

Time was flying, though, and soon Christmas was just a few short weeks away.

Megan was excited about an upcoming holiday party at Gabby's as well as a ski trip that she and Brice had planned. Her friend was just days from learning the sex of their baby and Megan was anxious to know if it would be a boy or a girl.

She was also considering adding on to her own family. Megan

wasn't sure if it was Brice's imminent departure that was fueling her, but she wanted to get another dog. Even though it had been just her and Lucy for quite some time, Megan still felt bad when Lucy wanted to play, and she was just too tired. Another dog would be company and a playmate. Lindsey and her mother both thought it was a wonderful idea and agreed that Lucy would benefit. Unfortunately, Megan had been so busy that she simply hadn't had any time to look. Hopefully, after the Christmas season, things would slow down, and she could really put herself to the task.

Megan had gone shopping with her mother and Lindsey for a dress for Gabby's party, since Lindsey as well as her parents were invited. The three women had decided to splurge and treat themselves to something new. Megan had noticed something different, however, with both her sister and mother. Whenever she tried to talk to them about Brice, they quickly changed the subject. She knew it couldn't be intentional, yet a part of her felt they were purposely avoiding any conversation about Brice which made no sense at all.

At the mall, they went to their favorite store and for the next hour tried on different outfits. Megan loved hanging out with them and more than once found herself collapsing with laughter. Later, they decided to go to lunch at a local restaurant, and upon arriving, dispensed with their winter gear, hanging jackets, gloves and hats over their chairs. After their food arrived, Megan decided to test her theory on their weirdness about Brice.

"I wanted to ask for your advice," she began, looking directly at both her mother and sister. "It's about Brice." Immediately, the two women exchanged a pointed look. Megan was now absolutely sure they were hiding something.

"Ok," Megan began, purposely placing her fork down, then

folding her hands firmly on her lap as she sat back to wait. "Spill it."

Lindsey looked terrified, as though all the hounds of hell were chasing her, while her mother dropped her spoon. Three times. In a row. Clearly, they were terrible at subterfuge. If she weren't so upset, it would be comical.

Lindsey spoke first, giving her mother a knowing look. Megan wondered if Lindsey even knew she could see her. Lindsey turned her full attention back to Megan. "I'm not sure what you mean, Megan. Spill what?"

Megan didn't buy her wide-eyed innocent look for a second. In fact, she knew she was hiding something. Turning her attention to her mother, she observed her folding and refolding her napkin with a great degree of attention to detail.

"Lindsey, I know you and Mom," Megan began, then, exasperated, turned her attention to her mother.

"Mom, stop playing with your napkin. No one needs a napkin folded that precisely, especially one they're using."

Glancing in her direction, her expression four football fields full of guilt, she placed the napkin off to the side, refusing to meet Megan's eyes.

Turning her attention once more to Lindsey, Megan simply stared at her and waited. Within seconds Lindsey began to fidget uncomfortably, then finally relented.

"Fine Megan, I'll tell you," Lindsey started as her mother placed her hand frantically on her arm, her expression clearly one of panic. Lindsey quietly assured her it would be fine.

"We're not hiding anything, Megan. It's just, well," and here she glanced back at her mother who quickly cast her eyes downward, "we know that Brice is leaving and that, well, you have said that he doesn't want to continue the relationship once he goes to Thailand, and the truth is—" here she took a deep breath, "the truth is we're just very angry with him," she finished breathlessly.

Stunned, Megan looked from one to the other.

"This is because you're mad at Brice?"

Nodding her head, Lindsey took a big gulp of water. Placing the glass down firmly, she continued.

"Yes, and so when you bring him up, we," pointing to their mother, "become uncomfortable."

"Yes," her mother chimed in, blinking rapidly. "Very uncomfortable, but Megan honey, if you really want to talk about him, we can listen, can't we Lindsey?" she inquired, her voice questioning.

Megan, her head ricocheting from Lindsey to her mother, was utterly confused. "Have you two lost your minds?"

"Of course not," Lindsey stated, her voice firm. "We just didn't know how to tell you that we were upset. I mean, you're going through a difficult time, so we didn't want to add to it," she finished, shrugging.

"But you were the one who told me to jump in, remember? You know, be brave and fearless and all that. So why would you be upset if Brice decides a long-distance relationship isn't for him?" she continued, raising an eyebrow. "Which, by the way, he hasn't actually told me. I guess I'm assuming on that one."

Shrugging, Lindsey took another large gulp of water, then another, then finished the glass entirely. "I guess I had just hoped he would change his mind about leaving, but, you know, he hasn't."

Something didn't quite ring true. Neither her mother nor her sister had ever held back their feelings before. Not in any situation, so she found it exceedingly strange that in the most important relationship she had ever had, they would choose now to remain silent.

Looking from one to the other she had no reason to believe they were lying, except, judging by her mother's nonstop blinking, along with Lindsey's desert thirst, Megan was positive that they were, indeed, lying. Sighing loudly, she picked up her fork, attacking her salad.

"I get it," Megan replied. "You love me, and you're concerned, but it isn't his fault. We never had an agreement. Brice has every right to follow his dream."

Clearing her throat, her mother responded.

"Yes Megan, I agree. Brice certainly has a right to his feelings and I for one will try to remain civil in his presence. We both will, won't we?" she questioned, turning her attention to Lindsey.

"Absolutely. We are here for you Megan and if you say we should try to understand Brice's side then we will. Definitely."

They finally finished lunch and afterwards Megan ran over the conversation in her mind. Something was still off; she just knew it.

# CHAPTER 13

The evening of Gabby's party arrived, and Megan was anxious to see her friend as well as take an opportunity to show off the incredible man on her arm. He had looked utterly delicious when Megan had opened the door, so much so that Megan had quickly ushered him into the bedroom, slamming the door closed with her foot. She had spent an hour taming her mass of curls, only to have Brice undo everything with his hands. Within moments they were naked, panting with need. Megan had taken the lead, pushing Brice backwards onto the bed as she straddled him. Bending, she had run her tongue slowly over his lips, arching as he had suddenly moved, taking her nipple into his mouth. She couldn't wait, as she reached down, pulling his hardness into her slick opening. Their climaxes were almost immediate, with Megan convulsing for long moments. When it was over, they lay entwined until Lucy began howling like a banshee at the door. Laughing, they had hurried to get ready again, neither one the least bit sorry for their late arrival.

Once at Gabby's, Megan was excited to see so many friendly

faces. Her parents, as well as Lindsey, were already there. Within moments of their arrival Sarah, whom Gabby had graciously invited at her request, rushed over to introduce her fiancé whom she clearly adored. They of course made a beautiful couple, and Megan was glad for the opportunity to get to know them better. She was shocked to see how much baby belly Gabby had and couldn't stop herself from placing her hand gently on the growing mound. When she felt the baby kick, Megan jumped back, shock as well as joy evident on her face.

Smiling widely, Gabby gave her friend a hug. "I'm so very, very happy for you, Megan." Puzzled by that statement, Megan stepped back and could have sworn she detected tears in Gabby's eyes but before she could question her, she was off to see her other guests. Shaking her head, Megan figured it was hormones and set about to enjoy her evening. There was so much food that neither Megan nor Brice knew where to begin but they managed to try just about everything. It was a lively gathering, full of Christmas cheer. Megan again marveled at how very fortunate she was to have so many wonderful people in her life. Glancing over, she observed Brice speaking with Sarah and her fiancé. Smiling inwardly, she wondered at how silly she had been to have ever felt jealousy. Megan, despite the loud party chatter, heard the doorbell in the distance. Glancing at her watch she was surprised. It was almost 10:30 which was a bit late to arrive for a party, she thought. Shrugging, she went in search of Brice who had disappeared while she had been catching up with an old college friend. Hearing a commotion behind her, she turned and froze.

Brice was walking towards her, Lucy by his side. In his arms he carried a large wicker basket with an enormous bow wrapped around it. His face was literally beaming, alight with joy. It was then that Megan realized a circle was forming around her. Lindsey, her parents, Gabby, they were all there, excitement shining from their eyes. By now Megan was utterly lost and immediately looked to Brice for comfort. Something was happening but Megan had no idea what it was.

Brice stepped forward, coming to stand in front of her. There was a hush throughout the room. Even the music had stopped. Looking up, Megan inhaled sharply at the stark love that was shining from Brice's eyes. He hid nothing from her. Placing the basket down, he untied the ribbon.

"I know this might have been very presumptuous of me," Brice began, "but I had it on good authority," here he looked pointedly at her mother and sister, both of whom were grinning widely, "that you were planning on doing this in the very near future, so I hope you love her." As the basket opened, Megan saw a tiny furry head peep over the edge. The creature had the brightest eyes and Lucy immediately walked over to it, licking its tiny face gently. Bending, Brice picked up the excited puppy. Megan had been rooted to the spot.

"Oh Brice," Megan gushed as he handed her the wriggling body, "she's beautiful!"

The new addition began licking Megan's face. Laughing, Megan looked over at Brice. His smile was beautiful, and Megan suddenly felt better about everything. Soon everyone came over to the precious bundle of fur. It was then that Megan realized why her mother and sister had been acting so strangely at lunch that day. They had been in on it all along! Embarrassed, she also remembered that she had been complaining about Brice at the time and here he had been planning this for her. The fact that Brice had clearly asked them what he could gift her with that would be special spoke volumes to Megan. No matter what happened, she thought, placing a kiss on the new puppy's head, she would always have a house full of love.

It had been a week since the newest bundle of joy had arrived, whom Megan had named Lilly, after one of her favorite flowers.

One evening, when Lindsey was visiting, Megan noticed suddenly that Lucy was in trouble. She was lying on her side, panting heavily and Megan knew she was in pain. Without thinking, she grabbed her and, sliding into her flip flops, ran for the door.

"I'm heading to the emergency clinic," she shouted, "Something is very wrong," and as much as she didn't want to panic, Megan felt terror rise, threatening to choke her.

"Wait," Lindsey called out, "I'll drive. You can't go alone." Together the two women raced to the emergency vet clinic, rushing through the door as they called for someone to help. Within seconds, one of the on-duty vets had Lucy in a room, examining her.

"I need to do some tests right away," he stated, his brows furrowed in concern. "We will draw some blood then do some x-rays." Megan nodded numbly, her stark fear constricting her airway. She had been stroking Lucy, whispering in her ear to be brave and strong and that she would be waiting when she came back. Lucy looked deep into her eyes and in them Megan could discern not only her love, but also her pain.

The sense of loss that she felt as she watched them take her away was excruciating. She felt her legs give way as Lindsey grabbed her arm, guiding her into the chair. Her anguish had a life of its own, pulsing into her bloodstream, drowning her. She felt Lindsey's hand grasp hers. Glancing over at her she could clearly see the pain etched on her face, too. Lindsey loved Lucy, and in that moment, Megan felt less alone. The two sisters sat this way for what seemed an eternity.

Megan had her head down, the tears coursing down her cheeks, unchecked. Suddenly she heard a deep familiar voice. Standing, she threw herself into Brice's arms, her tears becoming deep, hoarse sobs. He held her tightly, not speaking, only rubbing her back as she tried to gain some control.

"Has the doctor been back out yet?" he asked Lindsey,

speaking over Megan's head. She must have indicated no, and finally Megan turned her tear-stained face to his. It was almost her undoing. She could see how much this was hurting Brice, hurting all of them. They all loved Lucy and were all afraid. Pulling over another chair, Brice sat them both back down, holding her head against his shoulder. None of them spoke. Each had their own thoughts, each holding onto hope.

Finally, the doctor came out and all three stood, looking at him expectantly. His expression serious, he spoke. "It looks like she has a partial blockage in the stomach causing decreased blood flow. I'm afraid she will need surgery and we will need to proceed quickly." Megan couldn't understand what she could have possibly eaten and was wracking her brain as she signed the consent forms to allow them to treat Lucy. They had given her a sedative and the doctor assured them that she was comfortable at the moment. He wasn't sure how long the surgery would take but would give them an update as soon as he could.

Megan had no idea how she could have possibly managed getting through the next two hours without Brice and Lindsey. They were her support even though they, too, were worried sick. They each took turns pacing as the minutes ticked by. Megan thought of everything she and Lucy had done together, meant to each other and Megan knew, as she had always known, on that rainy day when she happened upon a small black bundle of fur, that it was she that had been saved. Lucy had saved her. In the myriad ways she had opened Megan's heart, she had shown her what unconditional love looked like. Lucy had listened to all her work stories, licked away all her tears. Touched the spaces that had been cracked and stitched them back. Bark by bark. And now, she could lose her. Though Megan knew that someday she would have to say goodbye, she could not accept that it was today. Not today. She was only a few years old, and Megan was determined to give her the longest life possible. "Not today," she whispered, her voice shaking.

Suddenly the door opened, and she instantly knew by the wide smile on the veterinarian's face that Lucy was going to live. In his hand he held a small rock that Lucy must have eaten on their walk to work, and Megan simply hadn't seen her. Relief flooded through her and all three of them hugged when the vet went back. Lucy would need to stay the night and since she would be sedated for many more hours Megan agreed to go home. She could pick her up first thing in the morning. After a final thank you from Megan and a promise to let her know how Lucy was in the morning, Lindsey left to go home.

The ride back with Brice was subdued. Megan was exhausted, both emotionally and physically and it occurred to her that Brice must be equally exhausted. It was 3 am by the time they arrived back and letting herself in, Megan allowed Brice to help her into bed. After stripping down, Brice climbed in, and she relaxed as he pulled her gently against him. With a satisfied sigh, Megan closed her eyes, a feeling of contentment washing over her. Within moments they were both fast asleep, Megan's last thoughts for the incredibly kind man that lay beside her.

Lucy came home the following morning and was still on pain medications for the next few days. Their reunion had been emotional and Lucy's joy upon seeing Megan had been an instant balm to her anxious heart. They were back home, and Lucy was curled up comfortably in her bed, snoring. Lilly seemed to sense that her friend was hurting, satisfied to lay beside her quietly. Everyone had been updated and Megan had decided to stay home since her assistant had offered to take care of the store. Brice had had to go to work early but would be over later that evening. A little later in the day, a bouquet of dog biscuits arrived, a gift from her parents. Laughing, she read the card addressed to Lucy, once again marveling at the joy she gave to so many lives.

Curling up on the couch with a cup of tea and her favorite blanket, Megan reflected on the amazing life she had and how incredibly grateful she was. The only shadow that lingered was the knowledge that very soon Brice would be gone. It had been nearly seven months since the day she and Lucy had crashed into his life and each day she fell deeper and deeper in love with him. The nights were steamy, sexy and hard. All she had to do was think of him and she was ready, all of her pulsing so that when he finally touched her, she was undone. She had never been more comfortable with another human being and at the thought of his absence she felt her spirit sink. So far, she had not allowed herself to dwell on his inevitable departure; however, it was closing in quickly. Still, she was determined to make the most of every minute. They were leaving for their ski trip in a few days and Megan couldn't wait. There remained no real mention of the future and Megan became increasingly anxious as to their definitive future plans, aware that Brice, while he loved her, had never actually said he would be willing to commit fully to a monogamous, long-distance relationship. That was not something she felt she could assume. Still, she had jumped fully in, so however this played out, she couldn't go back. She was in love with Brice. Going back wasn't an option.

Lindsey had offered to watch the store as well as Lucy and Lilly, sharing the store hours with Megan's assistant so they could take their ski trip. It would only be a few days as this was Megan's busiest season at the store and this year, she had double the orders from the previous year. Her books were no longer in the red and Megan was feeling especially celebratory, despite feeling guilty leaving all the incoming orders to fall on Lindsey's shoulders.

The morning of their departure arrived, and Megan and Brice were both excited. The trip to the lodge seemed to take forever but finally, they arrived. They quickly unpacked and headed to the slopes. The day was clear and just cold enough. It was a finely packed snow, perfect for a smooth run. Placing their goggles on, they jumped off the lift, quickly shoving off down the slope at the same time.

Megan was impressed with Brice's agility and together they were perfectly in sync. There weren't many other skiers so they both relished the abject beauty surrounding them. All they could hear was the swoosh swoosh of their skis as they raced towards the bottom. Once they finally arrived, both Brice and Megan were exhilarated. They couldn't wait to go again and after several more runs decided to take a break.

The lodge boasted a large great room that consisted of three giant fireplaces flanked by numerous chairs and couches. There was a bar area as well as hot cider and hot chocolate stations. They both opted for a hot chocolate and after grabbing their drinks settled into two overstuffed chairs that faced one of the fireplaces. For long moments they simply enjoyed being together as they sipped their drinks, each staring into the dancing flames, their thoughts a secret for now.

After a time, Brice glanced over at Megan, his face radiating happiness. "Have I told you today how beautiful you are?" he asked, sending her his sexiest wink. Feeling her body's immediate response, she leaned over the arm of her chair. Glancing around quickly to be sure they weren't being observed, Megan, ever so slowly, ran her tongue over her top lip. Brice's eyes widened and he immediately shifted in his chair. Leaning back once again, Megan knew she had his complete attention. In the guise of straightening her sweater, she let her hand caress her breast, then ran it down her body slowly. She could feel Brice's intense scrutiny. Feeling brazen, she took hold of the bottom of her scarf, tucking it between her legs, caressing herself as she took her hand away. Suddenly Brice bolted out of his chair. Grabbing her hand, he pulled her out of her chair. Laughing, Megan pointed backwards towards their still unfinished drinks.

"Wait," she giggled, as Brice continued to pull her impatiently towards the elevator, "what about our drinks?" Slamming the button on the elevator, Brice pulled her to him. His need was immediately evident, and Megan was just as ready as he was.

They fell into their room, stripping off their clothes as they made their way to the large bed. Throwing her down gently, Megan sank into the softness of the down comforter. The fireplace in their room was in full roar and Megan could hear it hissing and spitting as Brice spread her wide. His eyes were fierce, hot blooded. Megan thought he looked like an ancient warrior, virile, composed of hard planes. He looked directly into her eyes as he entered, one deep thrust that Megan welcomed with a cry, instinctively raising her hips to meet him. Teasing, he stopped, making her moan as he came in for a hot kiss, his mouth tasting of chocolate and lust.

It was well past nightfall when they finally were replete, snuggling before the fireplace, both wrapped in luxurious robes, sipping on champagne.

"I feel so very fortunate," Megan shared, as she looked around their suite. "It's so beautiful here and I feel like I need to keep pinching myself. Is this really my life?" she whispered.

"It's the beginning of our life," Brice replied, his expression warm. "Believe me," he continued, rising, then making his way to the small kitchen. "I had no real intention of a serious relationship when I moved here." Reaching inside the small refrigerator, he pulled out a small box that contained different types of chocolates. Brice had seen that they had every comfort and she felt sinfully spoiled as he leaned in for a kiss after handing her the box. Picking one, she popped it into her mouth, savoring the flavor as it melted onto her tongue. Brice had three to her one and laughing, it suddenly occurred to Megan that they had not had dinner. She realized she was famished and was just about to mention ordering something when there was a discreet knock at the door.

Glancing at Brice questioningly, he smiled.

"Food," he stated. "I called earlier, when you were napping."

"I wasn't napping," she replied indignantly, laughing at his wolfish grin. The waiter rolled the huge cart in. Megan had never seen so many covered dishes in her life and wondered for a moment if Brice was expecting company based on the amount of food he had ordered. Tipping the young man generously, Brice locked the door. Returning, he began taking the covers off.

Megan's eyes were like saucers as tray after tray of delicacies were revealed. Steak, seafood, potatoes, rice, all prepared by the amazing chef exactly as Brice had requested. "We are never going to eat all of this, Brice," Megan exclaimed, overwhelmed by the sheer amount before her. The delicious aromas wafting around her, however, caused her stomach to growl. Embarrassed, she reached quickly for a roll.

"Then again," she teased, "I might just be able to make a dent in all of this."

They both dug in with relish and when they were finally finished, Megan couldn't breathe. It had been delicious, and while she normally had a good appetite, this far exceeded her normal amount of food. They decided to stay in for the rest of the evening. After making love again in front of the fire, they lay in each other's arms completely sated. Brushing a kiss on Brice's cheek, Megan gently extricated herself, pulling the edge of their blanket up with her as she leaned against the couch.

"Brice," Megan began, "earlier you mentioned that when you moved here you had no intention of getting into a serious relationship. What did you mean exactly?"

Turning, Brice reclined on his side, his expression puzzled. "I don't think I really meant anything specific, just that I didn't think I was ready for marriage or anything too serious." Seeing her concerned expression, he rushed on. "But then I met you and that crazy bundle of fur," he continued, smiling happily, "and the rest, as they say, is history."

"I see," she responded, her expression reflective. "Brice, I love you and I know that you love me, but we haven't spoken of the future, and well, I think we should. Unless you were planning on just getting on that plane and never speaking to me again." Sitting up abruptly, Brice moved closer to Megan. Reaching out, he gently turned her face towards him.

"I haven't said anything because I wasn't sure what to say. I can't ask you to wait for two years, especially knowing that I can't travel back, and it would be incredibly difficult for you to travel there."

"I know," she replied quietly. "I guess the question we need to ask each other is would we be willing to have a long-distance relationship?"

Brice remained quiet for a few minutes; his mood pensive. She had hated to force the conversation, and while there had yet to be a definitive departure date set, she knew it was imminent. Megan needed to know where he stood. She needed to know if they had a future.

"Megan," Brice began, "I think we—"

Suddenly, Megan scrambled up, her hand covering her mouth as she raced towards the bedroom, slamming the bathroom door closed. Brice could hear her retching violently. Standing, he quickly put on his robe as he made his way to the door. She was clearly ill, and Brice was worried. Listening for a few minutes he waited until it was quiet and gently knocked on the door.

"Megan, can I help you? Do you need me to get you anything?"

Her muffled response came back. "No, just please leave me alone. I'm sorry Brice. I don't know what's making me so sick. Please just go to bed. I promise I will yell if I need anything."

Not fully convinced, Brice climbed into bed, staring at the door for the next half hour until finally it opened. Megan looked terrible. Her hair, tied back with an elastic, hung limply down her back. Her complexion was ashen. He watched as she made her way to the bed. As soon as she lay down, Brice curled up next to her.

"Are you feeling any better?" he asked gently. She nodded yes and he saw that her eyes were closed. Knowing she was exhausted, he turned off the bedside lamp. After reassuring himself that she was sleeping comfortably, he too drifted off.

# CHAPTER 14

The next morning Brice awoke to the sounds of Megan retching.

Immediately he decided that enough was enough and he was taking her to the hospital. Swinging his legs over the side of the bed, he was just about to stand, when the bathroom door opened. Brice thought she appeared so fragile, yet, despite her illness, incredibly beautiful. Megan made her way back to the bed, sitting on the edge as she glanced over at Brice, her expression downcast. He could see that she was fighting tears. Climbing back onto the bed he moved over to her, gathering her into his arms. Her shoulders shook as she cried quietly as Brice gently held her. Finally, only a few hiccups remained. "I've ruined the whole getaway," she sniffed, waving her hand weakly.

"You did all of this," her voice trailing off, as she moved out of his arms, resting her head against the headboard, "and I feel terrible that I got sick. I mean, I never get sick," she lamented, closing her eyes briefly. Facing her, Brice took her hand, gently rubbing her palm. It occurred to her that whenever she was upset, he would do the same thing. She found it oddly comforting, although, her other body parts, inevitably, began to respond as well. Keeping that to herself, she smiled wanly.

"Everyone gets sick Megan, it was just your turn," he finished pragmatically. "The question is how do you feel now?"

"I felt terrible when I woke up," she continued, nodding her head towards the bathroom, "but strangely enough I actually feel pretty good." Brice could hear the surprise in her voice, and he was relieved. It had come on suddenly and he really hadn't known what to think.

"I don't want to ruin the day," Megan stated, her expression determined. "I'm going to shower and maybe just have some crackers to start but we absolutely are going skiing today."

"Megan, that's not necessary. If you're still feeling off we can just hang here. It's pretty nice if I do say so myself," he stated, his eyes sweeping the opulent bedroom. The truth is, he had put a great deal of thought into everything and wanted this to be especially wonderful for Megan. Part of it, he knew, was the knowledge that he didn't know what their future held. They had started to talk about it last night when Megan had become ill and he was aware it was a conversation they needed to finish. Still, he wasn't looking forward to it. The fact that he loved her and that she loved him didn't take away from his worry about continuing the relationship when he was halfway around the globe. He knew he was ready to make that commitment but felt that unless Megan made it clear that it was her choice as well, he couldn't move forward with any plan for their future.

"I'm off for a shower," Megan announced, her eyes bright. "I actually feel amazing. I'm positive it was all the food I ate last night," she continued, as she jumped off the bed. Watching her head back towards the bathroom, Brice had to admit that she looked like herself once again. It must have been, as she stated, simply too much food.

"Do you want me to order anything for breakfast?" he asked. "Something light maybe?"

"I'm suddenly starving," Megan replied, surprise evident in her voice, "but yes, light would be best. Maybe just a bagel with coffee and some fresh fruit?"

"Done," Brice replied, as he climbed out of bed. A few minutes later he heard the shower start as he ordered their breakfast. He was determined that they would not get too serious today. "That would come soon enough," he thought, feeling trepidation. The future would just have to wait.

Returning home, both Brice and Megan found themselves busier than ever. The store was taking in a tremendous number of orders and Megan, for the first time, was able to offer her assistant full-time hours to help to get her through the busy holiday season.

She would sometimes be out delivering flowers well after dark and her time with Brice was suffering. That, and she was always exhausted. The minute she got home at night she would shower, make love quickly and be fast asleep within minutes.

As the time neared for Brice's departure, which he had been notified would come sometime in late January, Megan found herself feeling more and more restless. She was aware that they were both avoiding a serious conversation. Still, Megan wanted to wait until after Christmas to hear what Brice had to say.

The truth was, she was petrified that he simply did not want to continue with their relationship after he left and all of her felt broken at the thought. Megan had also decided it was time to see her physician about her constant fatigue. She knew it was her busy schedule and late evenings, but it had been over a year since her last visit and Megan had always been proactive about her health.

The Friday after they had returned from their ski trip, Megan had her appointment. After giving a urine sample she was ushered back to the exam room. Once there she began to feel a bit nervous. She was sure it wasn't anything serious, at least she hoped it wasn't, but she wasn't a fan of doctors' offices or hospitals.

She had only been waiting a few minutes when Dr. Lees walked in. Megan loved her. She was young, vibrant and definitely had her finger on the pulse of all the latest health news, especially when it came to women. Megan had started seeing her when she had turned eighteen and the two women genuinely liked one another.

Dr. Lees had her short blonde hair pulled back in a small ponytail. Under her white jacket she wore a bright red sweater over black business pants. Looking down, Megan smiled when she noticed her designer shoes. Megan knew that Veronica Lees had a thing for shoes. Smiling brightly, she gave Megan a quick hug and after a few pleasantries she set about to give Megan a thorough physical exam.

Afterwards, Veronica, leaning against the office wall, went into what Megan referred to as full doctor mode. Her expression serious, she asked Megan about some of her symptoms and after a few minutes took a rather deep breath.

"Well, I know what's causing your fatigue, Megan and it certainly isn't anything life threatening. Life changing perhaps," she continued, "but definitely not life threatening."

"Life changing?" Megan repeated, her expression puzzled.

"Megan, you're pregnant. Your urine sample tested positive. I'm going to order a blood test to be sure but you, my girl, are going to have a baby."

Megan just stared, unable to comprehend fully. Her heart racing, she took some deep breaths to attempt to quell the anxiety that threatened to overcome her completely.

"I don't see how that's possible. I mean I take birth control, and I know sometimes I forget, but no." Shaking her head back and forth she whispered, "No, no, no. There must be something else," she faltered. "Just, anything else."

Her expression sympathetic, Veronica walked the few steps to Megan, and bending, hugged her tightly. Standing, her kind eyes were directed into Megan's, now full of unshed tears.

"I take it this was unplanned," Veronica stated, her voice subdued.

"You have no idea how unplanned," Megan laughed, hysteria evident in her tone. "The father is leaving in a few weeks for two years. I don't even know if he wants children," she continued, her expression one of stark fear.

"Well, I'm afraid I can't tell you what to do Megan, however, as your physician, you will need to be seen regularly. For now, you can schedule an ultrasound and bloodwork before you leave, and Megan," she finished softly, "as a friend, give yourself some time to absorb this. Right now you're in shock but soon enough you will begin to think clearly, and you will know what is right for you. Whatever that is, know that I'm here." Megan jumped down from the exam table, hugging Veronica briefly. Stepping back, she drew in a deep breath.

"I have no idea what I'm going to do yet but thank you. I will definitely make the appointments and then I think I need to go home and, as you said, try to absorb the news."

After making all the necessary appointments, Megan drove home. She had been so consumed by her thoughts that she literally had no memory of the journey. Walking into her apartment, she slipped off her shoes as she tossed her keys onto the kitchen counter. Throwing herself onto the couch, she waited for Lucy and Lilly to jump up. Normally much more rambunctious, they seemed to sense her distress, opting to lay quietly beside her after she had given each their customary kiss.

Placing her hand tentatively on her flat stomach, Megan tried to imagine a life being formed there. A baby. Her and Brice's baby. Suddenly, she was overwhelmed with a fierce desire to protect this child, the life she carried within. Gently, she rubbed her stomach, allowing herself to feel joy, for Megan realized, unquestionably, that she wanted this baby, regardless of what happened between her and Brice.

Thinking about him, she remembered he would be home quite late tonight. His colleagues wanted to take him out to celebrate his upcoming trip and Megan found herself relieved. She needed time to think. She also needed to tell someone, so she quickly sent a text to Lindsey asking if she weren't busy would she stop by. Within mere seconds she responded affirmatively, asking if she needed her to pick anything up on the way. Megan assured her she had everything she needed, and Lindsey confirmed she was on the way. After changing into her favorite sweats and t-shirt, Megan made a cup of tea and sat, trying to figure out how she was going to tell her sister.

Her parents were a whole other nightmare. Not that Megan was afraid they would not support her, she knew intrinsically they would, as would Lindsey, but she hated the thought that maybe in some way they would be disappointed in her. She also worried about Gabby. The birth of her own baby was imminent, and she wondered how her friend would feel about her present circumstances. It was all too much to think about so Megan turned on the television hoping for something to distract her. Flipping through the channels, she finally gave up, turning the TV off. Instead, she sat silently, staring at her Christmas tree. It was three days away and normally Megan would be going from party to party, hanging with her friends, enjoying cocktails. She realized how much her life had changed in such a short period of time since meeting Brice and once again, placing her hand on her abdomen protectively, she wondered how much more change was to come.

Hearing the door open, Megan looked over as Lindsey walked in, kicking off her boots and hanging her jacket on the peg in record time. "It is freezing out there," she shivered, rubbing her hands together briskly. "I already miss summer," she continued, her voice resigned., Turning, she pointed out the window, "but that's about as far from summer as you can get."

Reaching the couch, she kissed Lucy and Lilly, both of whom were squirming with excitement. Jumping from the couch, they joined Lindsey as she sat across from Megan. Looking out, Megan realized it was snowing. She had been so distracted that she hadn't even noticed.

Lindsey tucked her long legs under her, sitting further back into the chair. "Just spill it Megan," her sister ordered. "I know you and you never ask me to come over out of the blue," When she saw Megan about to protest, raised her hand to silence her. "You always want me to bring you something. Always," she enunciated.

Sighing deeply, Megan gave a half laugh. "You have me there," she admitted, nervously running her hand through her hair. Suddenly, now that the moment was here, Megan was afraid.

Taking notice of the distraught expression on Megan's face, Lindsey sat forward, Lucy, followed by Lilly, forced to the floor. Casting insulted looks in her direction, they headed to their doggie bed, throwing themselves down with a snort.

"Something's wrong. What's wrong?" Lindsey asked, her expression anxious.

"I'm, well, I—" Megan trembled, then, taking another deep breath, she exhaled, "I'm pregnant. I found out today. I'm going to have a baby."

The silence was deafening. Lindsey blanched, her eyes blinking furiously. Opening her mouth to speak, she quickly closed it. Sitting forward, Lindsey clasped her hands tightly on her lap. Megan could see the tears in her eyes.

"First, are you healthy? I mean the doctor says you're healthy?"

Nodding affirmatively, Megan replied. "Yes. I mean I have to have bloodwork and an ultrasound but, I think everything is fine." Breathing a sigh of relief, Lindsey spoke, her voice thick with unshed tears.

"And you, Megan, are you alright? I can't imagine what you must be feeling."

Smiling, Megan's face lit with joy. "Oh Lindsey," she breathed, "I'm scared, and unsure, and terrified, and happy, and amazed, and all over the place but this baby," placing her hand gently on her stomach, "this baby is wanted."

Both women jumped up at the exact same moment, rushing into each other's arms. They cried together, their tears a combination of fear and joy, but mostly, joy. Stepping back, Lindsey looked at Megan's stomach, her face full of wonder.

"My niece or nephew is in there," she marveled. "I already love her," she finished, clapping her hands gleefully.

"Her?" Megan teased, raising an eyebrow in Lindsey's direction.

"Or him," she grinned, "but I have a feeling it's a girl," she finished, wagging her finger back and forth.

Laughing, the two sat down, allowing themselves a few minutes to simply digest all of their emotions. Soon though the subject became more serious.

"Have you told Brice yet," Lindsey asked, her tone pensive.

"No, I haven't, nor do I plan to."

Lindsey's expression revealed both shock as well as confusion.

"I don't understand. He's the father. Of course you're going to tell him!"

"No, I'm not," Megan insisted. "I have thought about it all day and it would only make him stay for the wrong reason. I mean, we have talked about our love for one another, however, he never confirmed that our relationship would continue past the time he leaves."

"But he didn't say it wouldn't either," Lindsey responded, her tone indignant. "You don't know how he feels."

"Not exactly, but I know Brice. He would withdraw from the program entirely if he knew. I'm aware from speaking to Sarah that after the first three months, contractually, they cannot. She explained to me that this is typical when you are engaging in medical services, at least that is how I understood it. So, I will tell him, but not before he goes. I won't do that to him, to his dream. Those people are suffering, Lindsey," she continued, seeing the alarmed expression on her sister's face. "It would be wrong."

"It's a mistake not telling him," Lindsey responded, angrier than Megan had seen her. The two rarely fought, but Megan could see how upset she was.

"I'm sorry you don't agree, but it's my decision, my choice to make." Turning, Megan walked into the kitchen. Opening the refrigerator, she grabbed a bottle of water. From the kitchen, her voice was strong, she was wholly intent on defending her decision.

"You know I love you," Lindsey called from the living room, her voice thick with emotion, "and I respect you as well. But you're wrong, Megan. This is all wrong. You have to at least give him a chance."

Suddenly, all the pent-up anxiety and frustration spilled out. Her voice choked; Megan exploded.

"I'm not asking for your opinion, Lindsey. I don't want it nor do I need it. It's really very simple. Brice will know soon enough that I have no intention of waiting two years for him. Period. And he will leave, and he will do great things and eventually we will have another conversation. But not now."

As she came out of the kitchen, Megan realized that Lindsey was staring toward the front door, a look of dread crossing her features. Gulping, Megan turned slowly. Brice stood as though frozen, his expression one of abject pain. Composing himself quickly, he spoke to Megan, his words harsh.

"Well, I guess that answers that, then," his laugh brittle. "Clearly you have made your decision. How fortuitous that I opted to skip my planned festivities tonight and instead join the woman I love for dinner." Swallowing hard, he finished, his anguish evident. "You can be sure from this moment forward; I won't make the same mistake." Turning, he ignored Megan's cry to wait, instead, slamming the door behind him.

Numb, Megan made her way to the couch, flinching when Lindsey tried to touch her. Sitting heavily, she stared blindly at the snow, now coming down in sheets. Somewhere, in between the cracks in her heart, Megan was able to appreciate how beautiful the lights were, illuminating the delicate flakes, each, she knew, an original creation.

"Please Megan," Lindsey begged, squatting down in front of her, tears streaking her face, "go after him. Tell him what you meant." But Megan was already shaking her head.

"I hate that I hurt him," she grieved, "but maybe it's for the best. I would have told him anyway," she continued, her pain evident, "not like that but, it still would have hurt." Suddenly she began to sob, Lindsey holding her tightly.

"Please don't be against me, Linz. I can't do this without you. Everything in me hurts. It's agony. More pain than I have ever known, but I must let him go. Please. Just be there for me."

Rocking her gently, Lindsey let her cry it out. She hated that Megan had made this choice. Everything in her believed it was wrong, but this was her sister and no matter what, she would stand beside her. Feeling a cold nose against her foot, Megan glanced down at Lucy, Lilly directly behind her.

"It's just going to be the four of us for a while," she whispered, her hand again covering her stomach. She fervently hoped it had been the right choice to make.

# CHAPTER 15

*I*t had been almost a month since she had spoken to Brice. It didn't feel right. It felt like grief. Megan stood, staring blindly out her apartment window, for once, the beauty of her surroundings failing to restore her. Instead, everything was a reminder of what she had given up. Placing her hand on her still flat stomach, she wondered again if she were doing the right thing. Her child, their child, deserved a mother and a father, yet, if she told Brice now, Megan could never reconcile whether he was staying for her or their baby.

She listened to Lilly and Lucy run circles behind her, their happy huffs filling the air. Turning slightly, she watched as Lilly, still much smaller than Lucy, attempted to pull a toy from her mouth. She had fallen so in love with her, as had Lucy, though it hurt Megan's heart when she remembered the love that had been so evident in Brice's eyes when he had handed the tiny wriggling bundle over. Their antics each day had been the only bright spot Megan had, yet, even so, it felt as though everything took so much more effort. She knew that her body was changing, that fatigue was normal, however, this was so much more, she thought. It felt as though she were walking under water, in the dark.

She knew that he was leaving for Thailand in three days' time, his departure date had finally been set for late January. She hoped she could remain strong enough to let him go. It was past the point that he could get out of his contract, so there really was no going back, Megan thought, morosely. She and Lindsey were speaking, but it was strained, something that had never happened between the two women before. Megan knew she had her support, just not her approval.

Hearing a soft knock, Megan's heart jumped. She worried each day that Brice would come over, convinced that if he did, she wouldn't be strong enough to turn him away again. Crossing to the door she sighed, then looked out the peephole. It was Amy. Taking a deep breath, she opened the door. Amy's smile was tremulous, her expression somber. Stepping back so she could enter, they both were distracted as Lucy and Lilly raced over to greet her. Bending, Amy rained kisses on both dogs before standing. Not speaking, she sat down, her hands clasped tightly together on her lap. They hadn't had any communication since she and Brice had broken up and Megan was petrified. She loved Amy, but she couldn't tell her about the baby. Not yet. Sitting across from her, Megan waited.

"You look awful," she began, her eyes sorrowful. "I'm not sure if that upsets me or makes me feel a little better. Brice looks worse," she finished quietly. She was staring directly into Megan's eyes. Unable to hide her pain, Megan closed hers briefly.

"I know," she replied quietly. "But we never spoke of the future, Amy. He never said he would wait for me for two years, so I guess I assumed it was over," she finished, shrugging, knowing it wasn't the whole truth. She had never given him a chance. The baby had happened.

"I feel like there's something else, Megan. Something you're not telling Brice. I have gone over this time and again. Brice has no idea that I'm here. He would kill me," she continued, "but I know you two love each other. It doesn't make sense."

Breathing deeply, Megan tried to control the tears that were lodged in her throat. Everything Amy was saying was the truth and the knowledge that Brice was hurting because of her was almost more than she could bear. But she remained stubbornly determined not to reveal the news of the pregnancy to Brice, at least not before he left.

Once gone, Megan knew that he couldn't come back. She was also aware that once he found out, she would lose Brice forever. He wouldn't see his child for almost a year after the birth. It would be unforgivable. But worse, Megan thought, would be to force him into a relationship with me he never intended would be forever. They all deserved better, especially their child, she thought.

With a determined voice Megan replied. "Amy, it's true that I love Brice, however, I'm simply not willing to wait two years for him. It's such a long time and what if I were to meet someone or he were to? It would be so much worse," she croaked, choking on the words. She would have waited for him forever she knew. But Amy mustn't know that.

Her expression angry, Amy stood abruptly.

"I see," she spit out. "I'm sorry I bothered you," she stated. Turning, she stalked to the door, flinging it open. "I completely misread who you really are. Perhaps it is for the best. You are not the woman for my brother." Without waiting for a response, she stepped out, closing the door quietly. Megan barely made it to the couch before breaking down completely. Amy hated her and Megan didn't blame her. She lay there crying for an hour, Lucy and Lilly staring up at her quietly.

Megan knew they were worried and so was she. This can't be good for the baby, she thought, sitting up. I cannot keep doing this. Standing, she prepared to get ready for work. I still have a business to run, a life to live. Still, she knew that every minute from now until she knew that Brice was gone would be filled with pain. "It's the right decision," she whispered. "It is."

The day that Brice left it rained all morning, then later, snow and sleet covered the roads. The sun never came out and Megan thought it was somehow fitting. Brice had tried to call her several times and once had stood outside her door. She had almost been undone but she didn't let him in. Megan had begged him to leave her alone through the door and he finally had. Despite the weather, she had a busy day at work with plenty to keep her occupied.

Later that evening, she was having dinner with her parents. It was time that they knew about their future grandchild. Megan was somewhat relieved that Lindsey, who had also been invited, would be unable to attend, although, her relationship with her sister had been better. The two had finally reconciled and Lindsey was excited about the baby, insisting most emphatically that it would be a girl. Megan didn't care, at least that is what she told herself. The truth is, she reflected, a son with dark hair and eyes that mirrored his or her father's often came to her mind. She had another ultrasound scheduled but did not want to know the sex of the child. She wanted to be surprised.

Arriving at her parents, Megan let herself in, slipping off her boots as she entered. Hanging her coat and hat on the coat rack in the entryway, she breathed deeply. "It smells amazing," she exclaimed, entering the large kitchen. Her mother had her back to her, stirring a pot of something divine. Megan gave her a quick hug before settling into one of the chairs placed at the wide center island. Grabbing some grapes out of the fruit bowl, Megan began chewing as she watched her mother create. Swallowing, she leaned onto the counter, her stomach growling.

"Let me guess," she said. "I would say, judging by the aromas, that you have made your infamous pot roast with red potatoes along with," here Megan sniffed the air loudly, "broccoli."

Laughing, her mother shook her head. "You would be correct, but you missed something."

"Really?" Puzzled, Megan sniffed again. "Hmmm. I give. What did I miss?"

Pointing to the oven, Elizabeth replied, "Yorkshire pudding of course!"

"Ohhhh yayyyyy!" 'Megan cheered, clapping enthusiastically.

Just then her father strolled in, his newspaper tucked under his arm. Megan was amused that her parents still had the newspaper delivered. She had explained that they could do the computer version, but her dad shook his head. "I like holding it in my hands," he had stated. "Turning the pages is part of the fun."

"What's all the noise in here?" he asked, coming over and planting a kiss on Megan's forehead. "I heard you both all the way on the other side of the house."

Both women smiled at him as he walked over, kissing his wife.

"Mom was just telling me what we were having for dinner and it's my favorite."

"Yes, I know," he answered, glancing over at her. "I had asked for my favorite, but she wouldn't do it. I guess we can all see who her favorite is," he finished, laughing.

Giving him a playful punch, Elizabeth announced that dinner was ready. After her mother served, they all sat together. The meal was delicious, however, Megan barely tasted anything. She had no idea how they would respond to her news. She knew that it wasn't the story they would have written for her, however, she hoped that they would be supportive. She needed her family more than ever.

After the kitchen was cleaned, they sat in the living room, facing the fireplace. For a few minutes none of them spoke, enjoying the crackling and sizzling light display. The room was cozy but not too warm. Megan found herself remembering another fire, in another room, as she made love to Brice. Instantly, she banished the image. It hurt to think about it. Sitting up straight, she cleared her throat.

Both of her parents glanced over as Megan attempted to push through the fear that threatened to overwhelm her. She loved her parents very much and the idea that they would be disappointed in her was more than she could bear. Closing her eyes for a brief moment, she began to speak.

"I have something very important to tell you both. I'm not sure how you will feel, but I hope you will be happy for me. I hope," she finished, quietly.

"You're leaving," her mother said, her tone resigned. "I knew it." Looking over at her husband, she continued. "I told you she would eventually go. The town's too small here."

"I don't think it is too small," her father replied, his tone indignant. "I mean our town maybe, but we're not far from Portland and that's quite big," he finished.

"There's not enough culture here," she continued. "You know, like New York, with all of their Broadway Shows. Is that where you're going?" her mother asked, swinging her head in Megan's direction.

"Wait, I'm not—"

"New York!" her father bellowed. "Why in the world would you go to New York, Megan? It's much too expensive and what about the store? Are you going to sell the store?" he finished, clearly incredulous at the thought.

"Wait, no! Stop," Megan exploded, her voice just a few degrees shy of hysterical. "I'm not moving! I love it here! What are you two talking about? I'm trying to tell you both that I'm pregnant for crying out loud. I'm pregnant and Brice is the father and he left today for Thailand for two years," she finished, completely drained. Seeing the shocked expression on their faces, Megan clapped her hand over her mouth, horrified by her outburst.

Myriad emotions passed over her parents' features. Within the silence she heard her heart beating through her chest, her father's fingers as they drummed on his armchair and the soft whoosh of the heater as it turned on. For a few moments no one spoke, then finally, her mother sat forward slightly, her expression a dichotomy of happiness and worry.

"I'm going to be a grandmother," Elizabeth whispered, the wonder evident in her voice as she glanced over at her husband. Megan's father still appeared dumbstruck, but he nodded, a soft smile lighting his features. Turning her attention to Megan, her mother spoke.

"I don't understand, Megan. Why would Brice leave for two years knowing he has a child on the way? That simply doesn't sound like the man we have come to know him to be."

"I would like to know the same thing," her father said, his displeasure clear.

"Well, I— that is, I mean, I didn't tell him. He left and he didn't know."

Megan's mother rocked back, stunned by her daughter's admission. At the same time, Megan heard her father's sharp intake of breath.

"Megan, why on earth would you keep that from him?" her mother asked, her tone bewildered.

Turning towards her father, Megan recoiled from the disappointment his expression held.

"I didn't want him to give up his dream," she explained, her voice subdued. "He never said that he would wait for me once he left for Thailand. If the reason he was willing to wait was because he loved me, well, that I could accept. But if he knew, if he knew about the baby," she finished, expelling a deep breath, "then I would never really know why."

Again, no one spoke and Megan, eyes downcast, felt completely lost. This had been the second time she had defended her reasoning for withholding the pregnancy news from Brice, except this time, when she heard herself speak the words, they carried less conviction. For the first time it occurred to Megan that she might have made a big mistake. Maybe the biggest mistake of her life.

She felt her parents as they sat beside her, her father taking one hand, her mother the other.

"Megan," her mother stressed, "your father and I love you unconditionally, and we already love this child. We have never interfered in your life and we will not do so now, however, we would both ask that you consider telling Brice as soon as possible. No matter what happened between you both, that baby, our grandchild, deserves the very best from you both."

Squeezing her hand, her father agreed. "We both love you and we of course care very deeply for Brice, as well as this baby. Your mother is right, Megan. Brice needs to be told. As a man I can tell you that he deserves an opportunity to decide for himself what would be best for him moving forward."

Megan allowed the tears to come, making no effort to hold them back. Suddenly, she was exhausted from all of it. It had been a whirlwind since she had first laid eyes on Brice and throughout, Megan had believed that she could handle whatever came her way. Yet, she realized suddenly that she had made a decision for Brice that she had no right making. None. He needed to know, and Megan knew that she had to tell him. She also knew that she loved him more than anything and that she wanted him, no matter how long that took. Her father got up and left the room, returning a few moments later with some tissue. Thanking him she watched as he made his way back to his chair and sat. Her mother continued to rub her back soothingly. Megan was overcome with love for their support. The news that she had just given them could not have been easy to hear, however, in their usual pragmatic style, they were absorbed and were ready to help in any way.

"I'm going to tell Brice soon," she promised. "He only just

arrived, and I would like to give him some time to acclimate. I just need to think of how best to tell him," she finished, her voice unsure.

"I know you will find the right words," her mother reassured her. "Now, with all of that said," she declared, her voice full of excitement. "Can I just say hurrah? Finally. I'm going to be a grandma!"

Laughing, Megan hugged her mother tightly.

She stayed a while longer, listening to her parents plan out the rest of their unborn grandchild's life, warmed by their unconditional love and acceptance. Now, she thought, comes the hard work. Telling Brice, she knew, could very well cost her the love of her life and the father of her child. Megan was stepping off another cliff, but this time she wondered if there would be anyone to catch her.

Contacting Brice turned out to be a much more difficult endeavor than she had anticipated. After leaving several messages on his phone asking him to call her, to which he never responded, she had finally managed to reach Sarah's fiancé, Ryan, to see if he could help her contact Brice. She assumed he could help since surely; he was able to speak with Sarah. Unfortunately, he had bad news.

"There isn't a way to reach them for the first twelve weeks," he explained. "They are off the grid, so to speak. No phones work out there, although they could possibly get through easier if they go into town."

"But why?" Megan asked, disappointment coursing through her. "What if there was an emergency?"

Shrugging, he replied, "It's a chance they take." They are working within a camp setting. Literally a series of large canvas tents that are set up in a forest area. The location is quite far removed from civilization as you and I know it to be. If you try to call, the messages will not get to voicemail. Skype would be the only option.

Clearly puzzled, he asked, "Didn't Brice tell you?" Without waiting for her response, he continued. "It was the first thing Sarah and I discussed. She was worried about it, but I told her to relax. That what she was doing was bigger than us. Although," he continued wistfully, "I miss her much more than I ever imagined. I bet you're feeling it as well," he finished sympathetically.

Realizing that he didn't know about their breakup, Megan decided not to say anything. If Brice hadn't shared that then he must have had a reason.

"Oh, I'm sure he mentioned it, but you know how it is," she responded nonchalantly, "life gets busy, and I must have simply forgotten. I'm sure he will reach out as soon as he can," she finished, closing her eyes briefly as she hung up.

"Three months," she thought, her heart sinking. She would be close to five months along by the time she would be able to reach him. Megan felt ill thinking about Brice's reaction. If she were him, she would never speak to her again. She thought she probably deserved it. How could I have ever believed that what I was doing was right? Well, now I have three months to think about that, she lamented. Placing her hand on their growing child, she could only hope that Brice could someday forgive her.

# CHAPTER 16

*B*rice couldn't stop thinking about Megan. He was literally in the middle of a rainforest, sitting on a giant log, far from civilization, yet it was as though she stood by his side. Brice missed her smile, the way her eyes sparkled when she laughed, her kindness. He could see her clearly in his mind's eye, especially at night before he fell asleep, exhausted. Then it was as though he could feel her, smell her. He allowed himself to remember how her hands felt on his body, how every inch of her tasted. Her eyes when he was above her, each thrust a declaration of his need for her. The flush that would cover her beautiful breasts, then rise, spreading across her features as she reached her pinnacle of pleasure. It was difficult to dwell upon, yet Brice was helpless to stop. He was in love with her still, though he knew that she didn't feel the same. When he had heard her tell Lindsey that she wouldn't wait, his dreams for their future had crashed down around him. Brice had no recollection of the seconds, or minutes or even the hours that followed that revelation. He had remained numb for days. She was the woman he wanted by his side for life, the woman he wanted to have his children with. He had believed that she felt the same way and would have bet money that she did. Although now he doubted he would have won. Still, their ending had bothered him, and he had wanted desperately to look into her eyes and for her to tell him that she didn't feel that way. That she truly wouldn't wait. It was an itch not scratched and Brice had tried to reach her over the weeks before he had left but she wouldn't see him. Devastated, he had almost been relieved when he had finally boarded the plane that would take him halfway around the world from her. He missed Lucy and Lilly. It was as though they were already a family and something close to hope nagged that maybe, just maybe, they could be.

"Penny for your thoughts," Sarah chirped playfully, as she sat down beside him. Startled from his daydreams, he laughed. "Give you three guesses," he replied sheepishly.

"Oh," Sarah replied, her expression sympathetic. "Megan?"

Nodding, Brice brushed his hand impatiently through his hair. "I keep telling myself to let it go but I can't quite seem to do that. It's as though my brain has accepted the end but my heart," his hand thumping his chest, "refuses to follow suit."

"I'm so sorry, Brice. I never really saw this coming either. I know what a woman in love looks like and Megan loved you. I was sure of it."

"Well, she might have," Brice answered, his voice bitter, "but not enough to wait. Call me old fashioned, he continued, but love, real love, does not have a timeline."

Thinking about her own situation and Ryan's sacrifice for her dream, Sarah had to agree, although she remained silent. It was clear that Brice was tormented. She had been playing with an idea but wasn't quite sure how Brice would feel about it. A longshot, but Sarah believed if it worked, then Brice might just have the happily ever after he deserved.

Taking a deep breath, she plunged in.

"Brice, I have an idea but first, I'm going to ask you a question.

I want you to really think about it before you answer. Really think about it."

Perplexed, Brice just stared at her, then shrugging, agreed. "Ok, he said. Go for it. What's your idea?"

"Well," she began slowly. "If I told you that there's a way that you could go back to Maine without breaking your contract and that you would be able to do so every three months for a period of four weeks each time, would you?"

Puzzled, Brice shook his head.

"Wait. So, every three months I could leave here, return to Maine for a month, then return here for another three months and so on until," he continued, waving his hand, "the two years are up?"

"Exactly," Sarah confirmed. "I guess what I'm asking, Brice, is do you believe that you might have a reason to return? Unfinished business perhaps?" her expression questioning.

Brice let the idea sink in, however, he was stunned to realize how quickly he knew that he wanted to do it. That he wanted an opportunity to see Megan again, to hear from her once more, this time looking into his eyes, that they were not worth fighting for. Just the idea of seeing her caused his body to react, his heart to begin a slow gallop. Brice knew there was a strong chance she would reject him again. He had no reason to believe that Megan had changed her mind, yet something about her demeanor the evening that he had overheard her conversation with Lindsey didn't feel right. Nothing she had ever said or done indicated that she didn't want to be with him. In fact, he told himself, he was convinced that her feelings for him were genuine. Then why, he wondered for the thousandth time, why wouldn't she even open the door when he had tried to speak with her? What could have caused such a sudden turn in her feelings? Shaking his head, he turned his attention to Sarah.

"I'm in," he stated, determination etched across his features. For better or worse, Brice would not give up on Megan or on his love for her. I'm going back, he thought, and I'm going to fight for her. I'm going to fight for us.

---

Megan had tried her best to stay calm as she waited to speak to Brice, however, it was always in the back of her mind that she would soon be breaking his heart for a second time. The three months were almost up, and Megan knew that soon he would see her messages and call. Knowing that he simply hadn't seen them told Megan that he hadn't been avoiding her. He might not like it, but she was sure he would call.

The past three months had been busy, for which Megan was eternally grateful. Work was better than ever, and Megan began looking at homes to purchase. Now that her family was growing, she needed a bigger place, so she had been out house hunting. Her budget was modest, however, her realtor Eva believed that she could find them the perfect residence. Today they were meeting at a small home just a few streets over from her parents. It was ideal, as Megan would need them to babysit, and Elizabeth Cunningham had already notified her employer, who was also her friend, that once the baby came, she would no longer be working. Megan hadn't even needed to ask. Even her father had a spring in his step, going on and on about sports events that they would watch together and how he would teach him to play golf. Of course, he assumed it was a boy. When Megan reminded him, it could just as easily be a girl, he had simply shrugged.

"Well girls love sports too and my granddaughter will be perfectly able to learn golf as well." Laughing, Megan shook her head. This baby was already so loved.

Megan had been present at the hospital when her goddaughter had made her grand entrance. She had never witnessed anything more beautiful than her friend holding this most precious child. Gabby had named her Elnora Ellsworth or

Nora for short, a tribute to the grandmother that had been so very treasured and so very much a mentor to Gabby before her death. It had also given Megan a glimpse into her own future, and she could only hope that she did as well as Gabby. Visiting her the previous day, she had marveled at how at ease Gabby was with Nora. It was as if she had always been a mother, so adept at handling a crying, hungry, wet baby without so much as a missed beat.

Watching her, Megan couldn't help feeling afraid. She would be a single parent. Even if Brice became a part of their baby's life, and everything in her knew he most certainly would be, it would still fall mostly on her shoulders. Still, she was more excited than afraid, and Gabby had embraced the news of her pregnancy with all of the love and the support of their beautiful friendship shining from her eyes. Holding Nora, feeding her, fascinated by her delicate features, had only made Megan more anxious to hold her own child. Their child.

Megan pulled into the driveway of the vacant home, parking behind Eva, her real estate agent. Megan had known her for years and had gone to school with her daughter. As she stepped out of the car, she knew instantly this was it. It was the saltbox style that Megan loved, with a wide wrap around porch. Two large Aspens banked either side of the home, a whitewashed cobblestone walkway leading up to the three-step porch. Along the base of the porch were flower boxes that Megan most certainly intended to utilize for her myriad flowers and plants.

As Eva opened the door, she smiled widely. "I really think you're going to love it." As soon as Megan stepped in, she knew she was home. It had an open floor plan with a giant white-washed brick fireplace at the center of the room. To the left, Megan could see a modern farmhouse style kitchen that boasted the latest in stainless steel appliances. There was a large master to the right with its own bathroom and a small hallway with another two bedrooms to the left. The floors were original to the home, which had been built in 1865. The ceilings were high, with stunning wood beams, also original to the home. There were floor to ceiling windows which allowed the rooms to be filled with an abundance of light. An inspection of the backyard proved to be just as amazing. It was large, with a six-foot fence surrounding all sides so she would be able to let Lucy and Lilly out with no fears. Here, there were several red spruce trees as well as a large mountain ash. Breathing deeply, Megan let out a satisfied sigh.

"Oh Eva, I just love it! I'm ready to make an offer right now but would like my father to tour it first if that's ok?"

"Absolutely," she beamed, happy that Megan loved the home.

"Could he come tomorrow?" Megan asked. "I'm anxious to get his opinion and get an offer in as soon as possible."

"Just have him call me," Eva replied, as they both walked back out to their cars. "I'm open, so anytime will work."

"I will," Megan responded, waving as she got into her car. Despite finding the right home, the drive back was dismal. I guess this is what they mean by bittersweet, she thought sadly. It should have been both of us here today. The thought hurt her heart all over again. A wound that was open and sore, Megan feared she would never feel whole again. Without Brice, she knew, there would always be a piece missing.

It was Friday night and Megan and Lindsey were doing their pizza and movie night. Lucy and Lilly had been racing through the house like crazy, jumping on and off the couch then the bed then the couch again. Over and over. Lilly adored Lucy and the two were inseparable. Lilly was smaller than Lucy's twenty-five pounds, her last weight coming in at just thirteen pounds. The shelter had been unsure of her lineage. Lilly had been one of eight puppies that needed to be rescued. Megan thought there might be some terrier because her chocolate and white fur stood straight up in tufts all over her tiny body, her bright eyes giving way to an expression of perpetual surprise.

Their antics were a much-needed distraction as at any time now she expected Brice to call. According to Ryan, he and Sarah should have arrived at the main camp yesterday. Megan had been watching her phone nonstop and finally, exasperated, Lindsey had tucked it in beside her on the overstuffed chair.

"A watched pot never boils," Lindsey recited, a phrase her mother had used many times over the years.

"Ugh, I know," Megan grumbled, aware that she was being obsessive.

"Have you thought about what you're going to say?" Lindsey asked, her expression curious.

"No, not really. I mean, I know what I have to say, but how, not so much."

"If I were you, I would just spit it out. Just say it and then zip it."

Rolling her eyes, Megan snickered.

"Spit it out? Can you imagine Brice calling and me answering, 'Oh, hi Brice. Yes, thank you for returning my call. I'm pregnant with your child and didn't tell you before you left. Also, I love you and cannot imagine my life without you so if you could just look past that last little thing that would be great.' I can imagine he would be just fine with that," she finished sarcastically.

"That is not what I meant, and you know it. I just meant you have a tendency, a habit if you will, of going the longest way around everything." Reacting to Megan's eye roll Lindsey continued. "You really do, Megan. Someone asked you the other day what breed Lucy was and despite not knowing yourself you took ten minutes to answer. I know it was ten minutes," she continued, pointing to her wristwatch, "because I actually timed you."

Megan started laughing halfway through Lindsey's diatribe because it was completely outrageous, and true.

"Ok you got me," Megan admitted, making room for Lucy and Lilly, who had both decided to lie on the couch with her.

"Seriously though, I just hope I say the right words, the ones that will hurt him the least. I have made a mess of all of this. I wish I hadn't been so stubborn, so sure that I knew what was best for everyone. Brice had a right to decide what was best for him. I cannot possibly hope for his forgiveness but I'm hoping anyway."

"We all make mistakes, Megan," Lindsey responded, her tone compassionate. "It's part of being a human. All you can do is try to convey to him the very best way that you know that you are truly regretful of your decision. It will be up to Brice whether or not he can find it in his heart to forgive you."

"I know, I know," Megan answered, her frustration evident. "The waiting is killing me though. I just hope he calls soon," she whispered, her hand resting on her abdomen. "My heart cannot take much more."

---

Brice stared at his phone, his heart beating wildly. Megan had called. His spirits literally soared as he anxiously listened to her skype messages. There was no reason given, just that she had something important she wanted to speak with him about. Once they had arrived back at the camp, he and Sarah had approached the camp advisor about their idea and had received approval for their plan. It couldn't have worked earlier because Ryan had never been cleared to join the program, but after speaking to a representative, the volunteer panel agreed to reconsider his request to join, finally agreeing. Basically, Sarah's fiancé would fly here to cover Brice, while Brice flew back to Maine to cover his practice. Ryan could spend time with Sarah, and he, well, he was counting on a petite fiery blonde to listen to reason. A simple solution and yet it had escaped everyone, except, thankfully, Sarah. There was a supply plane leaving in the morning and Brice decided he wasn't going to waste another minute. He would take the flight for the first leg of the journey, then a commercial flight the rest of the way home. He would be home by Saturday. Ultimately, he decided not to call Megan first. He wanted their initial conversation to be face to face. He knew it was a bit unfair to show up with no warning, but it was a day of reckoning and he was doing it his way this time. He would know, once and for all, if Megan was indeed the woman for him. Every single part of him was ready to find out.

# CHAPTER 17

Saturday morning was absolutely glorious except for the fact that Megan still had not heard back from Brice. Impatient, she had decided to try again last night but his phone had gone straight to voicemail. Frustrated, she had hung up, tossing and turning the rest of the evening. Despite being tired, she looked forward to her shopping trip with Lindsey and Gabby. It would be Gabby's first excursion without Nora. Megan had put in an offer on the house which had been accepted. Her father had agreed it would be perfect and had said he thought it had good bones, whatever that meant. Although the closing wasn't for another six weeks, Megan was anxious to have a few things put aside for the baby. Her mother was throwing her a baby shower, but Megan wanted to choose a few things herself. Something from her to her baby.

Thus far, the pregnancy had been perfect. Megan was just shy of five months along but was barely showing. She still fit in all her clothes, although her jeans did feel a bit snug today, she thought, as she made her way downtown. She would miss being able to walk to the store when she moved but the house was worth it. They all met in front of Megan's shop and after checking with her assistant that everything was under control, the three women set off. Although it was April, it was still very cool, and Megan wore a heavy sweater with a lightweight jacket. For the next two hours they shopped to their heart's content, although Megan had still not yet found that something special she was looking for. Hungry, they were making their way across the pavilion when Lindsey suddenly stopped, her expression one of stunned amazement. Wondering what had captured her attention, both she and Gabby glanced in the same direction and froze.

Standing in front of her store, leaning against the building looking powerful and altogether enticing, was Brice, one hand in his pocket, the other holding a beautiful bouquet of flowers. Her favorite flowers. From her store. His eyes captured hers and time, such as it exists, simply ceased. All Megan could hear was the sound of her heart, beating against her chest, her breath coming hard and fast. There was a deep warmth too, that slowly spread through her though she shivered inside her jacket. She watched, unable to move, as he pushed away and began to slowly walk towards her. Suddenly, she panicked. She wasn't ready! It wasn't what she had planned. Desperate, she looked over at Lindsey and Gabby. Though their expressions were sympathetic, they were also determined.

"You have this, Megan," Lindsey whispered in her ear. "I have faith in you. Just speak from your heart, sis." Megan watched as they both walked away and couldn't help wishing that people would start having way less faith in her. Brice stood directly in front of her, yet she couldn't seem to move her head, instead staring straight into his chest. She thought, somewhat hysterically, that this was where they had started on that day a lifetime ago when she had first charged into Brice's life, and his chest. Megan felt his hand lift her chin and she was immediately entombed in his eyes, those incredible eyes. She stumbled back from the intensity of the love she saw in them. How would she ever be able to tell him what she had done?

"What are you doing here?" she asked, clearly confused. "I don't understand."

"I know," he replied gently. "I was hoping to catch you at home, but I'm afraid you caught me. I bought you flowers." Megan smiled, as he handed her the bouquet. "I happen to know they're the best flowers in town."

Dipping her head, Megan inhaled their sweetness.

"Brice, could you please walk back with me? So we can talk?"

"I was hoping we could do just that," he said, taking hold of her cold hand. They walked quietly back to her apartment. Neither was prepared for Lucy's reaction when she saw Brice walk through the door. Her heartbreaking cry pulled at Megan's heart as she rolled all over him. Lilly jumped in as well and soon Brice was covered in doggie drool and fur. Megan could see the emotion that Brice held in check as he reunited with Lucy. Megan realized that he really loved her dogs, her heart hurting even more for what she was about to do.

Finally, Lucy and Lilly settled down, although Lucy would not leave Brice's side. Lilly went to her doggy bed, her bright eyes keeping them all in her sight.

Refusing anything to drink, Brice sat on the couch. Megan opted for the chair across from him. She couldn't trust herself not to just throw him down and have her way with him, something she had been replaying in her mind since the moment she had seen him.

"Megan, before you tell me whatever it is you wanted to say, please let me just know one thing."

"Brice, I—"

"Do you love me, Megan?"

His expression was so very hopeful, so very anxious.

Her expression softening, she whispered.

"Brice, yes I do, but—"

"Then why did you tell your sister you wouldn't wait for me? I don't understand how you could love me and say what you did."

Megan could see the pain etched on his features.

"Brice, there's something I have to tell you. That night, when you walked in—"

"Yes, I remember, Megan."

"Well, what you heard was only a piece of the conversation. I'm afraid, however, that when you hear all of it, you might walk right out that door and I will have lost you forever."

Shaking his head, Brice was clearly confused.

"What is it you need to tell me? Please, Megan," he pleaded, "I have spent the past four months torturing myself, wondering what I had done wrong, how I had failed us."

"Oh no, Brice. No. You didn't fail us, I did." Taking a deep breath, she continued.

"Brice, that night Lindsey and I were fighting. She was angry with me because I had planned the future for the both of us without giving you an opportunity to weigh in. It was so very wrong."

"A decision? About what? Megan, I'm afraid you're not making any sense."

"I know, please." Closing her eyes briefly, she swallowed hard. "Right before you were due to leave I found out. I'm—"

"Megan? You're what?"

"Brice, I'm pregnant. We're pregnant. I'm almost five months along."

Megan watched as waves of emotion crossed Brice's features, first shock, then joy and then anger. His attention focused on her. his eyes narrowed, mouth opening then closing. His hands were closed into tight fists and Megan was convinced she had lost him forever. "Brice, please say something," she whispered, her expression fearful.

"A baby? Our baby?" he repeated, shaking his head in disbelief.

"Please share with me how it is that you believed you had the right to withhold the information that I'm going to be a father," he spat out coldly.

Trembling, Megan answered. "I didn't want this baby to be the reason you stayed. I knew it was your dream to go so I—"

"My dream? You think that the existence of my first child wouldn't supersede a dream? A job? A car? A house? Anything else?" he bellowed.

Megan flinched, each word a sharp barb, slicing her already bleeding heart.

"No, Brice. I didn't think. I didn't think about anything, except that I didn't want the man I loved to stay for the wrong reason. If I told you I would never know, for sure, if I were enough or, it was the baby that kept you. It was utterly selfish and unkind, and I know," she whispered, "unforgivable."

"Why didn't you tell me that you would wait? There were plenty of opportunities, yet you said nothing. You acted as though my leaving was no big deal."

"That's not true," Megan sputtered. "I was devastated that you were leaving! Frankly," she continued, pointing directly at him, "it was you who acted as though it were nothing. How was I supposed to feel?" she finished. Then, standing abruptly, Megan walked over to him, hands placed firmly on her hips. "What about you, Brice?" she demanded. "Why didn't you tell me that you were willing to wait? Why did I have to be the one?"

Brice stood, forcing Megan to step back so she could look up at him.

"Because," he enunciated sarcastically, "I didn't want you to feel obligated to wait as well."

"Oh really? Well neither did I," she barked, both hands in fists by her sides.

"Well, you were wrong!"

"So were you!"

They stared at each other, Megan's breathing fast and shallow, Brice's deep and measured.

When he bent to kiss her, it was more than passion, more than want. It was like coming home, resting in that which was perfectly designed for you. It was a rapture of the mind, of the soul, an acceptance of all that would come. Megan felt Brice's lips leave hers but still he held her.

"We were both wrong, Megan. I allowed my pride to take over."

"I did too, Brice. I'm so very, very sorry," she whispered.

"We're getting married," he stated, his tone brooking no argument. Stepping back, he searched her face and smiled.

"I guess we could do that," Megan answered as she turned towards the bedroom. "But for now," she whispered, her voice husky, "I feel like we might have some catching up to do?" Waggling her eyebrows, she let out a squeal as Brice came after her, both tumbling onto the bed.

Desperate to feel each other, they ripped their clothes off impatiently, then Brice was over her. She could see the muscles in his arms pulsing as he held himself above her, then slowly lowered his head to her breasts. They were taut with need as she arched up towards him, impatient to feel him. Reaching down she held his hardness, his low groan vibrating in her ear. She tried to pull him inside of her, but he had other ideas. Reluctantly he pulled away from her grasp, then began a methodical onslaught with his tongue, moving slowly down her body. Megan was panting, sure that she would climax before he even touched her.

Suddenly, she wanted to be the one in control. Sitting up she backed away, listening as he growled impatiently. Grasping his shoulders, she pushed him down, her hair a canopy surrounding them as she kissed him deeply. Then it was her turn to slowly make her way, stopping to twirl her tongue around his nipples before licking her way down. She grasped him in her hand and she felt his convulsion, his breathing heavy. He was powerless to stop her. Her own body was on fire, demanding release but Megan was determined to give Brice all the pleasure that she could before seeking her own.

She met his eyes when she took him in her mouth, saw him clench his teeth as he fought for control. Slowly, she worked up and down until suddenly, he reached down to pull her up. Astride him, she slid him into her, taking all of him in. Her climax was immediate, Brice's only seconds from hers. She lay atop him for several minutes, then slowly rolled off. It would be many hours before they would finally leave the bed and then only to eat. Later that evening they fell asleep in each other's arms.

In the early morning hours, Megan was awakened by the feel of Brice as he gently moved his hand over her abdomen. Smiling, she went back to sleep, secure in the future that they were ready to create.

# CHAPTER 18

They were married in an old church that sat atop a hill. It had a wonderful, heavy, oak door studded with iron. Reticulated windows enclosed rich glass, allowing the sun to light Megan's path to her future. Brice stood, tall and outrageously handsome, his eyes never breaking from hers. Surrounded by family and friends they pledged everything that they had, all that they were to one another.

Later, they stood together in the churchyard, shaded by great elms that spread their majestic arms over all the wedding guests. Brice could not stop staring at his bride. Her dress, an empire design, did little to hide her pregnancy. It was early August, and their child was due in the next two weeks. They still had no idea if it would be a boy or a girl, but Brice didn't care. He had never known such happiness.

Sensing his stare, Megan looked over at him, her smile full of all that she had to give. Hearing a commotion, they looked over and observed Lucy and Lilly, both of whom had been flower girls, destroying one of the baskets that had held the rose petals. Lindsey was trying her best to wrest them away. Laughing, they knew there would always be chaos in their home. Brice had loved the house Megan had purchased. Sarah couldn't be here because Ryan was covering for Brice, but they had skyped from Thailand. They had become very close friends and Megan was anxious for their time overseas to be finished. Brice would still help those in need, just closer to home.

As Megan looked around at her family and friends, she was overcome with a deep sense of gratitude for all that she had. Her parents looked beautiful, her mother laughing up at something her father said, her face radiating happiness. Gabby stood by her husband, Nora between them, her thumb in her mouth. They were all so happy, so full of joy. Brice's parents, along with their spouses, all stood together, their conversation animated. Amy had brought her new boyfriend. Brice had shared that he wasn't too sure about him yet, but that he was working on it. Megan thought it simply couldn't be any more perfect, taking a deep breath.

Then, her eyes widening in horror, she looked down. Grabbing Brice's sleeve, she pointed. "Megan are you seriously telling me that our child is coming today?" he bellowed, staring in disbelief at the small puddle beginning to spread under Megan's feet. "Today?" he repeated, his voice incredulous.

Laughing, Megan nodded. "Looks like it," she answered, grimacing as her first contraction hit. Hard. She had read every baby book written and of course received advice from her mother and Gabby, but she hadn't anticipated their child would be early.

Feeling another one coming, Megan moaned. Suddenly, everyone was beside her. It was the very definition of chaos. They were all talking at the same time, so no one was really listening to her.

"I'm fine," she yelled over the cacophony, trying to reassure everyone as she began to walk slowly to their car. Her mother held one hand, Lindsey the other. Brice ran ahead to see if he could pull their car closer. Gabby kept telling her to breathe but she was already breathing. Amy was jumping up and down because she couldn't see over the crowd, which Megan thought was hilarious until another contraction hit, taking her breath away. Megan could feel the panic begin to rise as the pressure that she had felt earlier suddenly intensified. "This cannot be happening," she thought, hysterically. Then she saw Brice cutting through the mob towards her, not asking permission as he scooped her up in his arms. Everyone was scrambling to get to their vehicle when suddenly, Megan asked Brice to stop.

"Wait. Where are Lucy and Lilly?" she asked. Glancing over his shoulder, she couldn't see them anywhere.

"I'm not sure, Megan, but we have to go."

"Brice, no!" Megan cried. "I have to see Lucy! Please!"

Exasperated, he asked Lindsey to see if she could locate her and within minutes, Lindsey returned, breathless. "Amy has them. They are in their car, safe and sound. You can see her later Megan."

Relieved, Megan squeezed her eyes shut as another contraction hit.

"Brice, hurry," Megan breathed, her features tightening in pain.

Placing her gently in the front seat and buckling her in, he rushed to the driver's side. The car was moving before he had fully closed the door. The drive to the hospital took an eternity, although truthfully, it was a mere fifteen minutes away. There was a caravan of cars behind them, all racing to the same destination.

"Brice, I'm sorry," Megan panted, her pain now coming in waves. She had never felt anything like this and couldn't imagine why anyone in their right mind would ever willingly do this twice.

They finally arrived at the hospital. Megan waited as Brice went for help. Soon, hospital staff rushed out, quickly getting her into a wheelchair. She could hear everyone's well wishes as they started to bring her in, and turning, Megan could see Amy, standing with Lucy in her arms.

"Wait," she cried, "please." The nurse, confused, looked at Brice.

"Megan, we have to get you in."

"I know, I know," she repeated, waving at Amy. With a look of surprise, she rushed over. Reaching up, Megan touched Lucy's head, their eyes meeting. "Thank you, my girl," Megan whispered, "for everything." Nodding her head, the nurse began to wheel her in, an entourage of love following, as she prepared to take another giant leap of faith.

# EPILOGUE

*E*rik Michael Castillo came into the world weighing eight
pounds, four ounces. He had a head full of his father's
dark hair as well as his beautiful eyes. The delivery had been very
fast, especially for a first baby, for which Megan was especially
grateful. Immediately following the birth, she advised Brice that
she wanted at least three more. Brice agreed. They had stared at
him for hours, unable to believe how incredibly beautiful and
fragile he was. In the next twenty-four hours he would be held by
the people who would watch him grow, who would take him to
baseball games, who would teach him to read, who would kiss
away his tears, who would give him generations of wisdom.

He would grow to be taller than his father but the same height
as his two brothers. He would take care of his little sister, even
sharing with Brice the honor of walking her down the aisle when
she married. He would be the keeper of their family's history, the
storyteller, the rescuer of all things furry. He would name his
first dog after the one that watched him grow, the one that slept
by his side, the one he sought on dark days, the one who chased
him in play. Her name would be Lucy, the angel who rescued

them all, in one way or another. In the end, Megan lived all of her dreams and so much more, because, on a stormy day, on a deserted sidewalk, she reached out in love and received so much more in return.

# MEET THE AUTHOR

Darci Garcia is a contemporary romance writer with a penchant for including members of the animal kingdom in her stories. Although she studied business, her first love has always been the written word. She believes a sense of humor can cure almost anything and laughs at herself most of all. An animal rights activist, she has spent most of her life working behind the scenes assisting in the rescue of dogs. These days you will find her in sunny Florida, although she was born and raised in New England, which, she maintains, still holds her heart. She is living out her own happily ever after along with her husband, children and of course her rescues which, at last count, equaled five.